D0048831

Praise for *The Salt Fields*

"There's a beautiful formality to this writing that beckons a reader in, and then the vibrancy of the dialogue and the surreal allure of the scenes surprise and open up the story. A novella both stamped in time, and timeless. Flood has made something memorable here."

—Aimee Bender, author of
The Particular Sadness of Lemon Cake and
The Color Master

❋ ⚘ ❋

"Hyperreal yet hallucinatory, *The Salt Fields* fits a layered multigenerational saga into the fast-paced jaunt of a novella. A riveting story that mystifies even as more and more is revealed."

—Siel Ju, author of *Cake Time*

❋ ⚘ ❋

"*The Salt Fields* is a beautiful and powerful novella...with lyrical prose that had me spellbound from the first few sentences. Stacy D. Flood is a remarkable talent, and I can't wait for the world to know his name."

—Edan Lepucki, author of
Woman No. 17 and *California*

"Stacy Flood captures the feelings that arise in powerful and precise language, always up to the task. The birds that haunt the landscape and the momentary nuances of light are told as vividly as language can offer. The book is both tragic and beautiful."

—Maxine Chernoff, author of
Here, Camera, Under the Music, and *Bop*

❋ ⚓ ❋

"*The Salt Fields* is a gem—the kind of book you'll want to underline, dog-ear, study, teach, and beg your friends to read."

—Christina Clancy, author of
The Second Home and *Shoulder Season*

❋ ⚓ ❋

"Stacy Flood's first novella is a marvel.... *The Salt Fields* will stay with you long after the last page."

—Toni Mirosevich, author of *Pink Harvest*

THE SALT FIELDS

Stacy D. Flood

LANTERNFISH PRESS
Philadelphia

Lanternfish Press
399 Market Street, Suite 360
Philadelphia, PA 19106
lanternfishpress.com

Cover Design: Kimberly Glyder

Printed in the United States of America.
Library of Congress Control Number: 2020941239
Print ISBN: 978-1-941360-49-1
Digital ISBN: 978-1-941360-50-7

The Salt Fields

I'M OLD, SO HERE'S WHAT *you don't know yet, and what I don't want to still remember.*

From the time they were born, my father and uncle were taught that everything in the ocean was preserved in salt and everything beyond it was dead or dying or too far away to dream about. Everything on the other side, anything beyond the horizon, had disappeared or floated away distended and wasn't worth anyone ever remembering. They watched ripples pass along the surface of the water, and beyond these the trees along the mainland shore bent away from the winds.

What they knew of their home, a small island off the coast of South Carolina, was that it was sinking, receding, being devoured ever so slowly. While the men spent their time fishing, my father and uncle would circle the island in the late afternoons. My father became obsessed with sediment, my uncle with flotsam, and together they watched the tides rise and the reeds sink deeper, even against the cutting winds. Others in the town may have noticed this as well, but if so, they never mentioned it—maybe that was their collective secret; every community has one. They simply carried on with their lives as if the encroaching waters weren't something to be feared—or as if they were tired of fearing things altogether, since there was nowhere left to run. The shores narrowed and more shells were left behind when the waves did recede. The sea was claiming its territory once again.

Fifty years earlier: a slow curl, like a beckoning, which seemed to hover and pause, just for a second, before unfolding into a strike meeting skin. The air condensed and released, pop after pop, snap after snap, as each lash from the whip met flesh in staccato. The man flinched, flexed every muscle beneath each blow, as stripes of blood boiled up fresh atop each wound, and sweat ran down with stinging salt. He dropped to his knees, yet the ropes held him like tentacles, stretching his form between two trees as the air splintered again and again.

The man convulsed, a thin line of spittle hung from his lips, and his breathing thickened. There was a rush in his ears and sweat lined his face, dripping clear salt onto the cooling evening grass beneath him. Through blurred vision he could see his pregnant wife a few yards ahead of him, her mouth open and screaming, her knees digging into the tobacco-stained earth, her whole body angling towards her husband. A few of the older women held her back, leaning with all of their strength to keep her away.

But the strikes continued, blood-tipped lash, scarlet and wet, after blood-tipped lash, until there was little skin left to cut. His breathing slowed; his neck curled forward into his chest.

And his wife screamed: "Just let him die! For God's sake, just let him die!"

MY GRANDMOTHER WOULD TELL SUCH stories when I was small, to remind me that sometimes survival is relative. Some things we lose should be irreplaceable, and the thorns of the past or the future should always pierce the skin. That night, she said, as those lashes cracked against my grandfather's back, there was heat in the world but no longer any air. There was no longer oxygen or nitrogen, only heat. On every telling, I wanted to ask her whether my grandfather died that night, but I never did. He died eventually, one way or another—whether as the result of one single incident or the weight of them all together.

Throughout my youth I remember my grandmother being the woman people in town would go to when they wanted something to end. Young women—always with the most tragic of eyes and a tattered but clean shawl around their shoulders—would come to our back porch in the middle of the night. There would be whispers as light escaped the kitchen, and my grandmother would go inside, then return to the doorway with a green glass bottle that she would hand to the lone woman. Even beneath the songs of evening crickets I could only rustle the bed sheets so much without being detected. On the nights I stayed with her, and when those visitors came, I would pretend to be asleep and pull the quilt up over my face, drowning the shadows and sobs which darted across the night. I never really outgrew the comfort of that quilt. Years later, when I went off to college, it was the one possession that I was determined not to leave behind.

Without fail, a few days after a woman's visit, the people in the town would talk about how that very woman had, tragically, lost something nights earlier. I would often see those women's faces in the congregation the following Sundays, and they never looked happy, though some looked grateful or relieved. Some of them I never saw again. Mostly it was the darker-skinned women of the town who came to see my grandmother late at night. Unlike the lighter-skinned women, these darker ones sat in church alone, searching the crowd with lonesome eyes for some Biblical kindness, or they sat with their gaze cast downward—not in prayer, but as if they longed for something they knew they would never see in this lifetime, at least not with bodily eyes.

It made sense. Because who in their proper mind would want to bring a child into this world, raise him from wind and dust into this horror, only to be lesser than?

My grandmother had one daughter. On an island across the water there were two brothers, orphans, who were raised hard. Long hours of schooling, and beatings in order to release from their minds and from their blood any remnants of the curse into which they were born. The boys were objects, equipment, tools, insects, nobody's children, and many nights they would sneak away from the family that kept them and sleep clutching one another in a stranger's boat, whichever vessel had the heaviest tarp, as the winds roared above them and the waters below cracked, swayed, sizzled, and hissed. As they grew older they shivered less and less. On warmer days, when all you could smell was the sea, the two would sit side by side on the beach, blinded by the reflections from the waves, and watch the distant shore.

Until one afternoon the birds left. The fish jumped less. Dark clouds raced in to cover the sun and hide the moon. The boys measured the rushing winds and prepared themselves. My father packed a few books. My uncle slipped through the town taking as much money and canned food as he could steal and carry away in two pillow cases. Then, in the small hours of the morning, they pushed a boat into the water.

Once the brothers were drifting out from the shore, the sea rose further; the rains surged and slashed sideways, and lanterns were lit as the island's fishermen met the rush of water onto the streets and into their homes. My father could see chaos unfolding through the windows of the kitchens, where firelight flashed off streams of rain, but there were no other boats being prepared or launched.

The men came down to stand on the shore, some pointing towards the boat the brothers sailed in, but found themselves marooned there as the sea grew higher and higher.

My father couldn't hear any shouts or screams over the storm winds. Even when he turned to my uncle to ask a question, his words were ripped away, unheard, by the tumultuous air. My uncle stared stone-faced toward the distant shore they'd dreamed about their entire lives. My father returned his gaze to the island they'd left behind. The men on the shore were raising their lanterns higher, the women tightly clutching children and babies. In the patches of dim light he could also see the splintered pieces of other boats swirling on the waves—crushed and compacted by the storm, irretrievable.

While searching for food and money, my uncle had released every other boat on the island into the sea, which left each resident besides himself and his brother stranded: a dozen families left to drown in the enveloping night. Even through the distance and the drops of rain heavy on his eyelashes, my father could still see their tears.

As the brothers sailed farther away the lights dimmed behind them and brightened ahead. Jellyfish wide as dinner plates floated in the night waters beneath the small boat. My father turned away from his island one last time, never to look back.

Once the storm had broken, my uncle pronounced as he rowed: "They didn't love us, so we had to do this, you understand?" When my father didn't reply, he added—to convince himself and his own soul as well as my father: "If we didn't we would have drowned along with them, one day, one way or another."

❋ ⚓ ❋

The few townspeople who woke early that next morning saw my rain-soaked father wander up the main road. No one asked questions, as if no one had any right to. And as the town stared at him and his wet-pillowcase traveling bag, he walked into a small crawfish diner. There he asked if anyone was taking boarders and was at last taken in by a lonely couple glad to have a young man in their home to help with the chores, even one who had seemed to emerge from the sea like treasure.

He was alone. He and my uncle had agreed to part ways for fear their actions would be discovered. Even years later, my father claimed that he still thought of his brother every time the rain fell like daggers and exploded in puddles along the dirt roads.

They had split the stolen money evenly. My father kept his share hidden in a hollowed-out almanac that he read each night, since he would spend the remainder of his childhood mysterious and alone. Once older, he rented a tiny room in a boarding house one state away, which was the boarding house that my grandmother owned.

He grew up athletic, handsome, and God-fearing to a degree that no one could fully understand. Plus, he had money; no one questioned from where. My mother fell in love with him. They eventually married, bore one child, and then purchased one of the town's general stores.

Of his lost brother, my father heard distant stories: the young drifter with money and some talent with a pocketknife. They had promised to stay in touch as best they could, but fewer and fewer letters found their way back as the years moved forward. The last my father knew was that my uncle had headed farther west, reaching St. Louis before drinking up most of his share of loot. There he fell in love with a dancing girl, the daughter of an escaped slave, and the two of them headed to the left side of the continent, reaching Wyoming before the drinking got the best of them both. His wife died from winters when too much of the money went into shot glasses rather than firewood; from what my father heard, it was the type of cold that seeps into the bones so deeply that you can't get rid of it. She had left my uncle and moved into a boarding house a few weeks before it finally took her life. That was her triumph. Afterwards, my uncle traveled with the children of runaway slaves who had become cowboys since they were raised breaking horses. My uncle became something of an oil man and cowboy himself until the money was gone again and his bones became brittle and weary, and he was left to ride fence on an old horse, day after day, into the winter pastures where not a single blade of grass could reach through the thick, sharp snow.

My father always wondered if his brother had any children, and every time the door to his store would swing open and a dark-faced stranger would walk in, my father thought of the possibility that this was the niece or nephew he longed for, one loaded with stories of my uncle's well-being. When that new customer simply ordered a can of baking soda or condensed milk instead, my father always looked dejected, which made the town believe that he was generally more morose than he truly was. My father sent news westward along with any traveler he could find, anyone who was heading towards those mountains he'd only read about in magazines. He wanted to tell my uncle that all was forgiven, that no one had followed them from the island, and that there was a job at the general store if he wanted it. My father was convinced that word would reach his only brother eventually. It had to; that's how the world worked. You sent out what you expected from it, with enough heart and longing, and your reward came back to you. My father believed that. He had to.

Yet he used to dream every night of his brother's death through various tragedies—a tree falling on him, the earth beneath his feet simply giving way, a bullet shot through his temple as he lay sleeping against the cold earth. And after many years, on his own deathbed, with his eyes clouded and the fever winning, my father called out for his brother.

"Is he here? Is he dead yet?"

Everyone else around him thought that he was referring to me. I knew better.

But people also said that I'd gotten my wanderlust from this uncle I'd never met, even though I wouldn't say I had a lust for travel, rather an inner knowledge that I certainly didn't belong where I was. Throughout my childhood I was content, if not really happy; the latter seemed too much to ask for through the long hot days and sweltering nights. I had food, clothing, and friends with whom I shared marbles and tin toy cars, but I was the wealthiest, and it kept my friends distant. Best friends came, then moved away, and of the friends who remained, their parents remembered my father's mysterious arrival and my grandmother's mysterious late-night occupation—too well for them to allow their offspring to spend too much time with me. I understood and was content to keep mostly to myself. I think this saddened my mother a little, and to try to lighten my demeanor, my father would regale me with fantastic stories of his journey to our larger shore. I never believed in magic and wonder, so the tales were rarely successful; they only served as a reminder of his trials, real or imagined, versus my relative comfort.

As a young man I worked in my father's store, saved up my wages, and, since I never found anything else interesting enough to apply myself to, devoted my time to school, and eventually my money to college. I attended Morehouse, then transferred to Tuskegee, where I fell in love time and again—never deeply enough to hold my interest for very long. I wanted to be a physician—not a seeds-and-roots doctor like my grandmother but someone versed in all the interconnected systems of the body. When the money for my education dried up, however, faster than expected, I returned home to become a teacher and to marry a sweetheart I'd found more and more interesting as our summer friendships grew. We held hands, danced, shared Coca Cola and saltwater taffy on warm evenings, and held our first kiss for so long that time itself faded.

She broke it first and moved farther and farther away over the years, always accusing me of only seeing the edges of things, never the center or the whole or the heart. We had a daughter. Being an only child myself, I inherited the old family home after my mother passed. But when my daughter was three, my wife left us for another man, someone I hoped she'd found true love with. I understood: she had grown while I had not, and when I think of her leaving I imagine the two of us standing at the edge of a cliff, her growing wings and soaring into the sky while I stand on the edge, on my toes, watching, afraid to stretch any higher.

I think of her soaring and then I watch her fall. She was murdered later that summer, stabbed with a knife twenty-seven times. There were no suspects—not even the man she flew away with, who disappeared the day her body was found beneath crumpled bed sheets soaked with blood—and no investigation. This was the age when the murder of a Black woman didn't warrant the pay, ink, or gasoline that it would take to investigate, especially should the evidence lead to anyone other than a Black man. So the case simply got colder and colder, then frozen, until it drifted away like snow before her body was even buried.

✳ ⚓ ✳

"The Lord moves in mysterious ways," they told me, as their weathered, gnarled hands drifted from my shoulder to my tricep to my elbow, then away.

And for a year and a half after my wife died, my daughter and I were alone. Existing in that house through the seasons, she and I were pleasant enough to each other but never friends, or close. We worked the land together sometimes; she picked flowers rather than the weeds I asked her to, since she claimed that weeds were just wildflowers nobody loved yet. Her smile reminded me of her mother's too much and too often, so in return I smiled less, and by extension discouraged my daughter from smiling at all. We ate our meals mostly in silence, the whispering of the breeze louder than our words, and when the breezes turned into the cold winter winds, the crackling of the fire was the loudest sound in our house. We completed our chores dutifully. I never yelled at her, nor she at me. I listened to her sobs at night; she listened to me turn the pages of books I'd already read. We prayed, said what we were thankful for, and waited for something to break.

As light as her heart was, she broke next. Spring came quickly that year. She was eager to get out and play in the new grass and dandelions and burgeoning fields. She collected seeds in her pockets in hopes that the warmth of her skin would help them grow. She spent the warm evenings trying to collect fireflies, and as the sky softened to black, she would spell out her future by using the tip of her finger to connect one star to the next, her own form of celestial fortune telling.

There were few fences in town. Like dwellers in African deserts, everyone knew where their borders lay; they didn't need to be marked. My daughter went where she pleased. But she didn't notice the frost that had gathered so late in the year on the stones of the Richardsons' well. She climbed onto the edge, as she had done spring after spring, summer after summer of her youth, her small arms outstretched as if it were her time to soar.

Then she fell twenty feet through the darkness and died minutes after she reached the water below. Drowned. Usually, they say, it's the impact, the cold surface, that kills you—snaps the neck; you suffocate in another way. But the coroner told me that water had filled her lungs first, that she had drowned—or maybe that was the quickest answer and he was too lazy to look into things further. I imagined her slipping easily into the water and the darkness, letting it fill and envelop her, carrying her to her mother, carrying her home.

What alerted me that something was wrong that afternoon was the silence, the change in signal-to-noise; that stillness was different from what had shrouded us in previous months. Everyone thinks that all quiet is the same kind of emptiness, but it isn't. There's one type of quiet when you're hiding yourself and another type when the world is instead pulling away from you. I rushed to the well when I noticed the latter.

Maybe if I would have been even slightly more attentive as a father, she wouldn't have died, cold and alone in the dark. I'd learned to shut out her footsteps, her scratches, and the little songs she'd sing softly to herself throughout the day. I don't keep ghosts, but the silence from that moment has stayed with me forever.

I didn't go to her funeral. I made the arrangements, chose the casket and her finest dress, and purchased all the flowers, including her favorites (people wondered about the wildflowers and weeds), but I couldn't bring myself to attend. I thought it would be redundant: between my wife's memorial less than two years prior and my grandmother's obsession with funerals, to which I was her constant companion as a child, I was convinced that people were tired of seeing me at solemnities. I stayed at my job for the day. Walking home late that afternoon, I saw a flock of thrushes leap from the tall grass and rise towards the sunlight; as they turned in the sky, I was convinced this vision was all the religion I needed.

And although I didn't stop teaching, nor leave town, I drifted away. The days moved; I ate my meals alone, and no one spoke to me, the people of the town thinking me either cursed or tragic—both options equally flawed. The Richardsons' property and its well dried up after the place was sold, and eventually there were fewer and fewer children around for me to teach. I think everyone expected someone new to arrive, or someone from my past to return, to console me, to give me some morsel of wisdom or joie-de-vivre, but I didn't hold out much hope for that. Some nights I would buy a jar of white lightning moonshine and sit on the porch, watching the stretches of road in either direction for signs. Somewhere over the years I'd misplaced my father's almanac and the hole inside it filled with promise, and I spent long nights just waiting for someone to return it to me safe and full.

In the summer of 1947—amidst radiant poppies, citrus-tinged sunshine, and a clay-white sky—they found a mass grave in the next county. It was determined that it was an infant graveyard from the time of slavery, each skeleton curled into itself in a fetal position as if for warmth and protection. From that moment on I saw the ghost of my daughter all around me, day and night, in every periphery and shadow, and I could no longer sleep without calling her name. In the winds I heard her name, and I thought of the thrushes. In my memory, amongst the rustle of their wings, I now heard my daughter calling 'Daddy.' It was as if it took her own beloved spirit, released alongside those of so many who were buried before her, for me to realize how truly lonely I was and how much I wanted to see her face just once more.

It was then that I decided to leave, to travel north for the promise of great, steel-bending jobs and the opportunity for a different life, or at least fewer ghosts in the night air. I missed my daughter. I missed my wife. I missed my father. I missed my grandmother. And yet I had no desire to keep smelling the acrid detritus in the soil everywhere I stood.

Because, more than anything, I do believe in crossroads, and sometimes you have to heed their call no matter who you might meet there.

❋ ⚸ ❋

All the following week I had dreams of traveling—of the earth moving beneath my feet, then away from me—which the old folks in town always said was a sign you were going to die. But I think that in their dreams they found themselves collecting their belongings for a journey; in mine, I just left.

That Sunday I went to church and announced that I was selling my house and moving onward. I wasn't fearless, just determined. After the service a few parishioners inquired as to my asking price, and what time would be best for them to come by and take a look, but no one asked where I was heading or why. Also—and understandably, since most of the families in town were struggling to keep the little that they had—no serious offers came.

People disappear in the South, one way or another. In the Black sections it's rare when anyone goes searching for them, so I think it surprised the town that my departure was so deliberate, considering all the other mysterious possibilities. The Lawson family lived only a few houses away and had done so for most of my life. When the parents died, the oldest son took over the house with his wife and family, and they were kind to my new family, then my tragedy. There was a cottonwood in their backyard that I would climb when I was in grade school, but then one hard autumn a storm blew the tree over and it was cannibalized in order to keep the rest of the town warm.

Ronalda Lawson was only fourteen when she had a child with Oscar Wheatts, whose previous wife had died from pneumonia the year I went to college. Oscar had a car, which he polished as often as his days would allow, and a job in a car garage close to the white part of town, where he was respected as one of the best mechanics in town, Black or white. He had no children, and although at times he could be heard singing in the street after a night of drinking, he mostly kept to himself, clapped softly in church, and didn't mind being seen wiping a tear from his eye when a sermon touched his heart.

Oscar was free with his time and money, and since Ronalda's parents had nine children, he had the means to give Ronalda the kind of attention that her family could never afford. Ronalda wasn't very pretty, but she had a smile that could light up your soul.

There was never really any talk of the two getting married until the baby came, and then Oscar disappeared. Even though his car was gone, he'd left the rest of his belongings behind, which led some to believe there was a degree of foul play involved. Ronalda, though, was convinced he'd simply chosen the nearest breeze in the middle of the night and driven into it, then away.

I went to see Ronalda at her parents' house. For my visit the family set out an entire dinner, complete with a cobbler cooling on the windowsill; I think they half-expected me to invite Ronalda to leave with me. Throughout the meal Mrs. Lawson bounced her grandbaby on her lap. After dinner, I politely folded my linen napkin in front of me; at that small motion it seemed the entire house surged forward, waiting for me to speak.

"I'll be leaving town soon," I said.

"You'll be missed," Mr. Lawson lied, while Mrs. Lawson went to the bureau to pull out a box of cigars. "The school has never seen a finer teacher."

"Thank you." Though it was insincere, the compliment made me uneasy, and I took a sip of water to collect my composure. "I've been trying to get rid of my house," I continued, moving the crumbs from my biscuit around my plate while the youngest Lawson girl cleared the porcelain gravy boat and the pitcher of iced tea from the table.

"That has always been a fine house," Mrs. Lawson said. "Your wife, Lord keep her soul, kept that house so nice. And every year she would plant those posies in the front yard. They were so pretty. And the roses. Beautiful. She had a way with them. I still don't know how she got those roses to bloom that way."

"Your wife was a fine woman," Mr. Lawson interjected.

"Yes, she was," Mrs. Lawson added. "Your daughter was a fine child, too. Poor thing."

"I've been trying to get rid of the house," I repeated. "But I haven't gotten any good offers."

"Well, money's kind of tight around here," Mr. Lawson said. He crossed his legs; only then did I notice his freshly polished spats. "But that new mill should open up soon. What you could do..."

"I was wondering," I interrupted, "if Ronalda would be interested in taking the place for me. Free of charge, of course. The stove is good and there's no draft through the floor or the walls. All the pots are sturdy and clean, and the plants are still alive. And the flowers."

The room fell to a silence where you could hear the breeze in the curtains and the bumblebees buzzing in the afternoon light—each casting a tiny shadow as it passed, then disappearing.

✿ ‡ ✿

The morning I left, as I was packing, I saw Ronalda walking up the road to my house in her finest dress, a melding of crinoline and cornflower-blue linen, carrying two suitcases. I met her at the door and apologized for not having left sooner; that morning I'd slept longer than I anticipated or wanted to, as if there were, after so much pain, a peacefulness in the house that I wanted to collect and take with me. She smiled that wonderful smile and in turn apologized for arriving so soon. I immediately gave her the keys. I didn't ask where her baby was.

So we worked around each other as the sun crept upward through an azure sky. I packed as much as I could—my grandmother's quilt, a rose petal from the garden, more than I thought I would need—into my only suitcase, which was designed more for style than transport. While unpacking her few things, Ronalda straightened the items I was leaving behind. We spoke little but smiled when we passed by each other, and from the wistfulness in her eyes it seemed that she would have rather left with me than acquired a lonely house free of charge. I packed what was left of last evening's cornbread and spare ribs into my tin lunch pail, and when I was ready to leave I told her goodbye; she kissed me on the cheek and, without saying a word, went back to refolding the linen in the china closet, now all hers.

I wore my best pin-striped suit to the railway station, with the same chestnut and white two-toned spats that I'd worn to my graduation and wedding. In the front breast pocket I placed a small photograph of my daughter—crumpled at the edges, creased across the middle. I hadn't realized how much weight I'd lost until I wrapped that suit around me and tied a loose half-Windsor knot into my tie. The suit itself was fawn in color—linen, with cloud-white pinstripes, totally wrong for my complexion, I'd been told—but it was comfortable, and for me it represented the chrysalis from which I was to emerge.

Once I descended the three stairs from the front porch to the concrete walkway, the other steps came quickly. I meant to turn around for one last look, but by the time I thought to do so I was over a block away and couldn't see the house anymore.

From there I kept walking—past sunflowers, fields of wilted grass, bales of autumn hay, even the Richardson property—without breaking stride. The farther I walked, the more the colors around me softened. By now, though, most of the farms were little more than sand and rotting plywood. The only voices were cicadas that fell silent as I approached and began their whispers again when I had passed. At the edge of my vision I saw the well—the police had warned us not to use the water for a few days after they'd removed my daughter's body because, sometimes, a body can contaminate the supply. Sometimes some of the skin stays behind.

The emptiness in my suit allowed for a degree of cushioning against the sun; my heels scrapped against the bone-pale, dead-white dust and loose rocks, and for the first time in my life I couldn't find a rhythm to my steps. I didn't whistle, nor hum, and my mouth dried, my throat grew parched, and that was okay with me, since I couldn't find a single reason why I'd ever need to speak again. For those I'd left behind I knew my voice was already a memory, and I knew that this place, my home, would forget about the rest of me as soon as my shoes left the pebbles beneath them.

※ ☦ ※

Even when I was a child, trains never held much fascination for me, and as an adult I'd never bought into the romance or mysticism that said they could take me to a utopia beyond my current vision. I just needed one to take me to someplace slightly better, far away, where I could try to forget the rest of myself and replace it with whatever was around me.

The railway station was obscured by swirls of dry afternoon and glazed sunlight. Cars edged into the parking lot, the hum of their engines choking in dust, following ruts formed by similar slim white tires, and entire families emerged, each in their Sunday best, prepared for destinations elsewhere. Each of us collected there that morning, young and old alike, had a vision of the North as some sort of paradise, so we were dressed accordingly. Yet all the people, even whites, held a sense of regret on their faces, as if this quest for a new life signified a failure in or desertion of their old. Handkerchiefs wiped foreheads and were held in front of mouths as suitcases were carried inside. People squinted towards the sun for a heavenly answer as to why they were being roasted on what might be their last day in South Carolina. Young men smoked cigarettes. Old white men patrolled the entrance, looking for sharecroppers to stop and harass, but once my eyes met theirs they let me pass freely enough; I was less important to them than even I imagined. Tap dancers, some younger than my lost child, shuffled for change or ceremony.

Romanesque pillars stood in the front of the main, whites-only entrance—freshly painted, with flecks of dirt caught in the ridges carved to look classical and permanent. The colored entrance was along the side of the station, closer to the actual tracks, where the paint chipped and exposed the pine flesh beneath.

There was a single common platform, dense with sweat and anticipation. I tucked my suitcase under my arm and presented my ticket to the porter—a stout, dark man who lived in one of the adjoining cities, and whose cousin once owned the local pharmacy. We didn't acknowledge each other, though, as if already I was distant and transformed into someone new, someone he didn't recognize.

As crowded as the bench was, I was able to squeeze onto the edge and, like the rest of the occupants, turn my head expectantly toward the direction in which the train would arrive. Although I held no admiration for the machines themselves, what I've always liked about train tracks is the way they converge on the horizon and give the impression that someday, inevitably, pleasantly, the future will come to a fixed point, a sharp metallic conclusion. They give the illusion that whatever is lost can easily be replaced by distance.

In less than an hour that horizon was broken by a tall, thin cloud of smoke. Children in tall, thin socks and patent-leather shoes, polished enough to show perfect reflections of the families around them, raced to the edge of the platform for a closer look. As the lone black dot neared, adults began gathering their belongings. Rather than a grinding, we heard a squeaking of metal and a crunching of sand. Rather than anticipation, there was a feeling of resolve. When I looked towards the front of the station platform I saw a young white woman—she didn't appear older than seventeen—sitting still on a cast iron bench amongst the commotion. Even though she was visibly pregnant, no one helped her, and when another porter tried, she ignored him and instead squinted forward, away from the train, into nothingness, waiting. I turned my glance downward.

By the time the Dawn Lightning rolled into the station I'd mopped the sweat from my neck, brow, and palms, and had counted the splintering planks on the platform floor at least a dozen times. I counted the nails which attached them at least a dozen more. Atop the plank closest to me, a maelstrom of ants circled something invisible. People rose and stood in line to board; I stayed on the bench a moment longer, watching pigtails bounce above the bright-wide eyes of small children excited for their longtime dream of a train ride to come true. Their mothers and fathers followed in thick shawls worn over summer dresses and suit coats over frayed suspenders or coveralls: moth-eaten, too heavy for the hot weather, but the easiest way to transport what one owned. When I looked for the young pregnant woman, she was gone; only then did I board the train myself.

Perhaps I should have waited a little longer. When I entered my appointed car the aisles were still crowded with travelers waiting for others to make a decision. Baggage was stacked to the sides and around us, as if taking priority over the passengers. I searched for familiar faces, not expecting or finding any, and then took the nearest available seat—on the aisle, facing the rest of the car and the back of the train, so that I could only see where I'd been, which was fine since I didn't really care where I was headed—and placed my suitcase in my lap. I imagined others were watching me, but they weren't. Somewhere a baby cried and was silenced. Across the Pullman coach, in a window seat, sat a small boy, hair cut close to the scalp, with a suitcase in his lap and a crinkled newspaper opened to the comics section. He didn't acknowledge anyone at all, only stared out the window as if longing for home. The station filled the windows closest to me; beyond the windows across the aisle was an open field with hills I'd memorized too early in life to find them impressive now. This container was my world for now, and beyond its walls there was a well I wanted to forget. I sank into the thin upholstery as much as I could, breathing the stifling air as slowly as possible, savoring my share. I wanted to ease into sleep and dream another life until I arrived at a location where I could actually build one.

The first thing I noticed was the uniform. I'd seen an Army uniform before, but usually on paler skin, or partially constructed—an Army shirt with blue jeans or Army trousers with a white T-shirt. I'd see the wearer holding a bottle of Coca Cola or a glass of iced tea on a late summer afternoon, surrounded by family members celebrating his return. Carvall, however, wore his full dress uniform—hat, tie, and all—which made the other passengers pause a moment and take notice. In turn, Carvall seemed uncomfortable with the attention, which might have been why he chose to sit down right next to me instead of taking advantage of the empty bench that faced us. He slid his duffel bag beneath the seat, then removed his hat and placed it on his lap.

"Man, if I only knew that it was going to be this hot today," he said to what I first assumed was no one in particular. "Glad to be leaving? I think I am, too. Especially on days like today."

"Where are you from?" I asked. I'm not usually interested in conversation, but the anticipation of our departure made me a little nervous, and I was longing to pass the time until the train actually moved us away, as if, at any moment, a cop or spirit or storm could come and trap us here in a pile of bruises or thick mud or regret. Talking, I figured, might keep the clouds and mists, or at least idle time, away.

"Florida," he answered. "But I was stationed down in Mississippi." He folded up his hat and stuffed it into his pocket. "Where are you heading?"

My eyes fell to my hands. "All the way to the end. Pittsburgh. Buffalo maybe."

"Me, too. I plan on getting a good job up there and never look back. Steel mill. Milkman. I don't care." After wiping his palms against his trousers, as if preparing himself for a day's work, Carvall extended his hand and properly introduced himself. He had broad hands, scratched as those of someone who'd worked in the field, and an enormous, luminous, straight smile. I didn't ask about his Army rank, or if Carvall was his first or last name. "Going to get me some respect, too," he continued. "That's important. Yes, sir. Those Negroes in the Army taught me that, the ones from the North. They *demand* respect."

"My name's Minister," I said as we shook hands.

"Minister?"

"Yes."

"Was your father a minister?" he asked.

"No." I could tell he was surprised by my answer.

"Did they want *you* to be a minister?"

"Not that they mentioned."

"So why did they name you Minister?"

"I'm not sure." To me it was just a name, and I'd never thought about it much. "Never had a reason to ask." Before Carvall had a chance to respond, I added, "Maybe they thought it was regal."

"Ain't nothing regal about any of the ministers I know."

"Maybe they thought I needed the Lord."

Carvall stared at me for a while before smiling. "Well, I knew guys named Deacon so I guess it's about the same, huh." I smiled back. "The guys at the base used to make fun of my name. They said I got my name because my daddy was probably a 'car full' of niggas. Get it? Car full?"

We both laughed. "So, Minister, what do they call you for short?"

"Nothing, really. People rarely use my first name, and if they do, they rarely say it more than once."

"Why? You important or something?"

"I don't think so."

He pulled a packet of gum from his uniform pocket and, realizing it was empty, crumpled it back into his pocket. "So no nickname?"

"Nope."

"What do your own people call you? The people who know you."

I didn't want to talk about my family and hoped he didn't ask about any friends. I thought about my daughter, lying here deep in the southern earth, and about who would take care of her when I was gone. "I'm not sure."

"Shit, even ghosts have names." Carvall settled himself into the seat with a renewed purpose. "Well, then, that's what we'll do. By the end of this train ride we'll find you a decent name."

I expected him to loosen his tie in preparation for the long journey, but instead he straightened it and looked out the window closest to us, searching its contents for a solution to the equation that was me.

❊ ⚓ ❊

Divinion and Lanah were the last two people to settle their things, although I'd seen them enter the train long before I did; they switched seats multiple times before selecting the last two in the coach, the ones across from Carvall and me. Like many of the passengers they were dressed in their First Sunday best, but their First Sunday apparel was of higher quality than many of us were fortunate enough to own—Divinion wore a tie that seemed to change in hue and pattern as you watched it, and Lanah flaunted strand after strand of white pearls, which shimmered a watery blue under the right glint of the sun, resplendent. She was stunning in a beige dress with cream lace and accents. Lanah was lighter-skinned, Divinion darker; the two complemented each other. Divinion removed his fedora and wiped his handkerchief across his brow, while Lanah waited some time to take off her wide-brimmed hat. When she finally did, I noticed that she had mesmerizing eyes, whose liquid hazelnut brilliance exuded clarity of soul. Once they were settled—Divinion by the window, Lanah on the aisle with a small valise on her lap—Carvall introduced himself and stretched his hand out to Divinion, who shook it with the same warmth that was offered before introducing himself and his wife.

"Where did you serve?" Divinion asked.

Before Carvall had a chance to answer, Lanah asked me, "Do you know how long this trip is going to take?"

"They say about a day," I answered.

"About a day," she repeated to Divinion.

"It'll be over sooner than you think," Divinion replied.

Lanah then reached a gloved hand into her purse, pulled out two wrapped pieces of hard candy, gave one to Divinion, and opened the other for herself. She placed the candy on her tongue, looked away from all of us through the window across the aisle, and waited until the train pulled away from the station—into the expanding sunlight, away from the station's shadow and gravity—to swallow. I looked out the same window, towards the shrinking platform, curious as to what interested her so much, because all I saw was a chaos of insects and ash and tin cans filled with tobacco spittle rusting in the sun. I saw a woman standing at the station counter trying to purchase a ticket. An old man sat on a bench near the platform, staring intently in the direction the train had traveled from, as if he were waiting for something else, something better, to follow.

The train rattled, metal jolting metal, as cinders and traces of coal streaked the windows—each flake the color of pepper, carrying its sharp scent throughout the coach; you had to blink through the fog of heat, noise, sweat, and conversation to maintain your bearings. Unlike Divinion, I wiped my brow with the back of my hand for fear that my handkerchief would never dry.

We were moving, but on that platform that old man's gaze didn't change. We were on the only daily train; no others would follow. What was he waiting for? My father? My uncle? A slave ship? A tall ship? Something ancient to return? But there was only smoke.

We were like the nautical travelers of ages ago, headed

towards the edge of the earth, unconcerned with falling over. All we had was faith and what we could barely see beside or behind us, but we were eager for change, anything different, even drowning. By the next morning we would be reborn. Deep down, many of us didn't trust or believe the newspapers and store catalogues that had promised a better life hundreds of miles colder. Many of those who'd traveled north before us had never returned, or we'd never heard from them again. As far as we knew, we were heading straight for the precipice, into salvation or perdition, and we were fine with either.

※ ⚓ ※

We were in motion for fifteen minutes before Divinion introduced himself to me as well, and then Lanah followed suit. It was not a lack of openness or politeness; it seemed that Carvall and Divinion had formed a quick rapport around which Lanah and I circled. Divinion hadn't served in the military but at one time had worked for the WPA out west and afterwards found himself fascinated with any portion of America that wasn't the South. He'd returned eager to leave the South again, and when the opportunity to move north and make a comfortable living in the steel mills presented itself, he bought one-way tickets for himself and his new wife.

"Chance to see more of this big world, you know," Divinion announced. He mentioned that he had family close to our train's route.

I thought again of the family I'd left safely buried in the holy earth. I wanted to tell him about my uncle out west, just to enter the circle that was forming between him and Carvall, but before I spoke I realized that all I had was the myth of adventure, nothing certain, and nothing that I could claim as my own.

We exchanged overviews of our family genealogy to see if there was a blood connection between us, but oddly enough we couldn't find any. Nonetheless, we agreed to consider each other cousins for the duration of our time together, as much to cement the bond we'd formed among ourselves as to shut others out of our burgeoning conversation.

"Were you overseas?" Lanah asked Carvall. "I have family overseas."

"Yes, ma'am, I was in France."

She straightened her back. "France? Why, that's where my family is from."

"I didn't see too much of it, though."

I wanted to ask Lanah what family she had in France, where I imagined clear blue skies cut by swifts or the contrails of war machines, but instead I skipped ahead in my thoughts and asked Carvall, "Did you see any airplanes shot down?"

"What?" he asked in reply.

Before I had a chance to explain—I'd only seen a few airplanes by then, and I wanted to know how quickly something so magical could fall through the cold, damp air—Divinion waved his hand dismissively and leaned forward to ask: "You make it with any of those French girls? I heard..."

"Divinion," Lanah interrupted, as Carvall just smiled; yet she looked at him as if waiting for an answer.

"Okay, okay," Divinion laughed. "They let you kill any white people?"

"I sure tried."

This time the two laughed together, Divinion slapping Carvall on the knee as he leaned into his hard-backed seat. I didn't join in, not because I didn't want to but because my focus was still on explaining myself, formulating my question in a better way. By that time Divinion and Carvall had moved on, and they made the subsequent conversation their own private joke, impenetrable, cultivated over easy time. Lanah kept staring at Carvall for a while, then looked over at me and smiled, as if my silence were an attempt to prove that I was above it all. She was right: I was hiding the part of me that wanted to join the camaraderie and brotherhood. I could admit that only to myself, though, and begrudgingly.

Divinion smacked his lips. "Hell, no white man is ever going to let a nigga kill another white man, German or not. White folks are too smart to start that shit."

"Still, I tried." They laughed again.

"I bet you did, brother," Divinion said. "I bet you did."

Lanah leaned forward into the mottled sunlight and asked, "Did you keep your gun?"

With a sly, bashful grin Carvall acknowledged the innuendo, which Divinion felt obligated to punctuate by asking, "Which gun do you mean, honey?" Lanah smirked as Divinion laughed at his own joke.

Lanah leaned in even closer and gave Carvall an even slyer smile. "Did you keep your black pistol?"

"Why are you getting personal with that man?" Divinion protested. When the three of us just ignored him, he added, "Maybe he got it shot off?" He turned to Carvall. "You get it shot off?"

"Can I see it?" Lanah whispered.

"Goodness, now you want to see the man's gun?" Divinion asked.

"Yes," Lanah answered without looking at him, continuing her game, piercing Carvall slowly with her stare. "I want to see that long. Hard. Black. Steel. Gun." She was savoring each morsel of Carvall's discomfort, as if every one of his uncomfortable swallows were a ripened delicacy. She smiled even broader as she noticed, then savored, the same discomfort in me.

Saving us both, Divinion erupted into another burst of laughter—nervous, perhaps, but just as boisterous as true laughter would have been—and shook his head. "Now you know they ain't give no nigga no gun. Barely let him leave with the one he come in with. You mean more like a wash pail. Or a fry pan. Or a mop. A floppy mop. That's all they gave niggas in the service."

Lanah leaned back in her seat and allowed her husband to change the subject.

From then on they talked freely amongst themselves but little to me, as if I were only an observer and not as interesting as I fashioned myself to be initially. In turn, I shared little, kept quiet, opened my lunch pail, and ate last night's leftovers as the minutes passed. On the road to the station I'd realized that I hadn't brought a book or a newspaper with me, but I'd decided not to return for one—not that I expected conversation on my journey, maybe just a little wonderment to keep me occupied. Instead, I spent the time stealing as many glances at Lanah as each moment offered, then looking out at the high dust of the South Carolina afternoon, watching for butterflies as the sunlight coated the fields.

The rattling of cargo and bones was punctuated by the train bell as we approached stations, about one every hour, where more passengers got on board but few disembarked. There were two bells as we approached, three as we were to depart. Each stop could last half an hour, or sometimes what felt like several hours, as people and luggage were crammed inside or on top. There were cardboard boxes filled with cracked porcelain, and dime store jewels only precious for the memory of the souls who'd once worn them. I watched porters and engineers walk along the sides of the coach—one on the platform, the other on the tracks—and grimace. I turned to look behind me, hoping to see beyond the passengers to the front of the train.

Each coach filled with more souls; some stood, but few talked, fewer laughed, and no one else entered our row, which I attributed to the sharp look Lanah gave any man, woman, or child who tried. It was as if she'd chosen her court, and no one else needed attend. A little boy in a suit stared at her for a moment, mesmerized, before looking to me for an explanation of who she was and why she was on a train like this with us. As an answer, she produced a folding Chinese fan—black lacquered to look expensive, with red silk and gold embroidered cranes—and opened it with a flourish, then lazily waved it as a comfort and a shield between herself and the others.

"I could have ridden first class," she finally admitted.

"What? Lord knows I paid enough for these tickets here," Divinion replied.

"I could have." She had the complexion and demeanor for it.

"Now, Lanah," Divinion began again.

"I could have walked right up there to that ticket counter, spoke a little French."

"You know French?" I asked, finding my voice again.

"Barely," Divinion tried to answer for her.

"Enough," Lanah replied.

"How do you know what's enough?" Divinion turned to me. "She learned some from this old Creole boy."

"Still, it was French."

"They probably speak something completely different over in France."

"French is French. As far as those crackers know. Those white folks would have let me right in." She adjusted her gloves as if that, along with the gloves themselves, were proof. "Except you stopped me."

"They would have stopped you."

Lanah shook her head. "Maybe, but they didn't, *you* stopped me."

"We would have been apart, honey," Divinion added.

"You can take care of yourself for a little while, can't you?" Lanah wasn't interested in his answer. "Doesn't matter now. But that's the problem. Black men are always trying to keep Black women down. Trying to tell them what they can and can't do, only because they can or can't do it themselves."

"That's what you think."

"It's true. Y'all just feel small so you try to make us feel small, too."

"Small to who?"

"To every white man y'all see."

"That's a lie."

"Deny it all you want."

"I ain't never felt small to a white man my entire life."

"Honey, you were born feeling that way. You just got used to it."

"You ever seen what those crackers can do? Really do?"

"They're just men," Carvall interjected.

"No, sir," Divinion continued. "Real men don't do what I've seen, do that to another person. I've seen the bodies of Black folks swinging from the trees, all charred with the skin falling off. I've walked miles of roads at night where they left dead Black boys to rot in the dirt along the side. That is, what pieces of those boys were left. An arm here. An arm there. Just left for the crows."

"And you kept walking." Lanah added.

"What?"

"You didn't do anything but keep walking. You just walked away."

"What would you have had me do?" Again, Divinion waved his dismissal. "You don't know what you're talking about." He pulled Lanah closer to him and smiled. "Besides, walked right into you, didn't I?"

"Hm," was all she answered.

"And I took you with me."

"Ain't nothing special about white folks," Carvall said again. "They're just men."

"What are you saying?" Divinion countered.

"I fought with them," Carvall said.

"You did not."

"Well, not with them. Beside them. They are just people."

Divinion sat back in the chair. "No, sir. I disagree with you there. They are not just people."

"Are we really debating whether white men are truly men?" I finally had to ask. "They are. They are carbon and corpuscle just like we are, just like everyone on this train is."

"Oh, and you know this because you've spent so much time with them. You know this because you've studied. No, I don't think so. You say this because that is the way you want it to be." Divinion leaned in closer. "You ever cut one? You ever watch one die?"

"They die," Carvall said.

"Shit, they die. I know they die. I seen them die. But they don't die the same as you and me. Their bodies die, but they pass that money and that power onto their children so, in a way, they live on. They don't just fade away like Black folks do, with maybe a couple of dimes and some fucked up stories to their name. No, white folks live on."

"So you're talking about ghosts," said Lanah. "Niggas are always talking about ghosts."

"Ain't nobody..."

"Apparitions and shit. Scared of ghosts. Niggas always scared of something."

"Ain't nobody talking about ghosts, woman." Divinion said. "You can get rid of ghosts with a few words and roots. What I'm talking about is forever." He sat back in his chair as if the rest of his story was familiar to us. "See, your Daddy..."

"Don't you talk about my Daddy," Lanah interrupted.

"Like most of the people here's fathers, drank up their money, and when they died ended up like dust fading away.

White folks? Their pasts take root, grow into them. They ain't people. I don't know what you call them."

He sat back further in his seat and crossed his legs as the sun rose high into the afternoon, as if, with that, his point was final. Eventually he closed his eyes with a deliberate air, placed his fedora over his face, like there was nothing left in the world for him to see, and soon he drifted asleep in a way that defined a level of comfort no one else in that train car had shown—mouth open, frame slumped, sweat dripping down the curve of his neck only to be absorbed by his shirt collar. For a couple of hours the train didn't stop. All the while, Divinion kept his head on Lanah's shoulder, as if she was the most precious thing he'd ever owned and he wanted to make sure everyone saw, and that no one stole her in his slumber, or that she didn't steal herself away. Lanah kept silent and precise, adjusting her dress now and then to prevent wrinkles. If she dozed off, he would imme-diately wake up, as if they slept in shifts—either for protec-tion or to minimize the time they spent with one another.

Carvall wrote letters for most of the early afternoon; I didn't ask to whom. He scribbled with his pencil as the sky slid to dry blue, then bleached milk-white, and he kept writing through the tatters of sunlight and the passing pine groves. Eventually the pencil fell from his hand as he began snoring slightly, so I picked it up and placed it on the seat beside him before it had the chance to roll away.

After a few minutes it seemed as if the entire car was in slumber, as if the train itself was propelled by the momentum of our dreams. I rarely sleep, since my dreams are mostly memories or nightmares; often I just close my eyes and try to find images in the darkness that remains. From where I was sitting, I couldn't see much of the sky, so I tried to make shapes from reflections and shadows instead. I listened for insects hitting the other side of the glass, and even through the clack of the wheels I could hear the din of workers and farmers in the fields beyond—if not actual sounds, then my memory of them. I thought I heard singing. The rest of the coach drifted in and out of sleep, afloat like ships at sea. A few passengers snored, their rhythms uninterrupted by the train's occasional lurches. A few children played, and in the heat of the day people ignored them, left them to their fun, since no one was sure what the future held for any of us. I watched Lanah. In every flash of sunlight she sparkled like the brightest jewel I could imagine. She was the most elegant creature I'd ever met, embodying the refinement and subtle gracefulness I hoped to find up north. When she slept, she slept upright, still, hands and long fingers crossed on her lap, gloves folded atop her collapsed fan. Her fingernails were painted the color of dried blood.

I blinked, closed my eyes for what I swore was only a second, and opened them to the swaying of the coach. Lanah was staring directly at me, waving the open fan in an even rhythm, careful to direct the resulting breeze at herself alone. She kept her gaze constant, even as a sly smile spread across her face, and as much as I wanted to look away, I had no excuse for avoiding it. I was trapped, so I let her stare wash over me. I started to like it.

I smiled. "I wasn't snoring, was I?"

She shook her head. "When is your birthday?"

"Excuse me?"

"Is today your birthday? People usually make these big decisions near their birthdays."

"Is it your birthday?"

She squinted. "I asked you first." I stayed silent. "And is that really your name?"

"Minister?" I added an apologetic smirk. "Yes. Minister Peters."

"Sounds like a slave name. Like Hero. Or New Boy."

"It's just a name."

"Well, are you?" she asked then.

"Am I what?"

"A minister. You don't seem like one."

I laughed because it was the second time I'd heard that question on this train, compounded by the many times I'd heard it before. "No. My parents were just optimistic."

"I don't know," she replied. "I've never met a good minister in my life." She opened her purse. "You got a cigarette?"

"I don't smoke."

She then sighed. "Divinion smokes, but he counts his cigarettes. I've never met a man so small, have you?" She didn't wait for my answer. "I'm not even sure where he keeps them. He doesn't believe a woman should smoke." She searched her purse for a moment longer, then returned her glance to me. "Do you believe a woman should smoke?"

"I don't have much of an opinion on that, ma'am."

Then she laughed. "Well, Mr. Peters, if you don't have opinions on anything as simple as that we're going to have a long trip together."

"Minister."

"Minister Peters."

When I think back on that moment nowadays I remember her smiling when she repeated my full name, but it could have been a reaction I imagined—something in the half-life of the early afternoon, those moments of dilated pupils, the silent world, and stillness. I imagined her staring into my eyes and smiling, she and I in some kind of contest to see whose eyelids could stay open and alert, who would blink the most, and who would slip into dreams first, whatever dreams we might find. We watched each other, suspicious animals, in the heat of the rising day.

※ ⚓ ※

Sunlight burst into our car as the train's doors lurched open at the next stop, and I awoke to the sound of voices that were now familiar. I opened my eyes when I heard Carvall reply that he was "fine, thank you."

"Man, you practically have a rug on your head," Divinion countered.

"I do not," said Carvall. Noticing that I was now awake, they both turned to me.

"Now, Minister's hair looks all right," Divinion said before returning his focus to Carvall. "But, boy, I thought the military made you all keep your hair looking good."

"Ain't nothing wrong with my hair," Carvall replied.

Divinion turned to his wife. "Lanah?"

"You need a haircut," she replied without looking at any of us.

"And this is the stop to do it in," Divinion proclaimed. "Right down the road. Take no time at all." He leaned towards Carvall and me and spoke a little quieter. "Besides, there's some numbers..."

"There it is," Carvall interrupted.

"Let me finish."

"How are you going to play the numbers in some small town you may not make it back through?" Carvall asked.

"Oh, if I win I'm making sure someone gets my money. I got enough family nearby to check." Divinion sat a little straighter in his seat. "Besides, it would be good to stretch our legs a bit."

Carvall sighed. "Yeah, that's true." He stood. "Lanah, you want to join us?"

Divinion slapped him on the shoulder. "What's wrong with you?"

"What?"

"You don't bring no woman to no barber shop."

"I know that. I meant just for the walk."

"No, thank you," she finally replied. "Minister promised

to take me to lunch." She smiled at me, and I tried to hide my surprise.

Divinion didn't hide his surprise in the least. "When did y'all discuss this?"

"While you were asleep. I was thinking that little catfish place we heard so much about. Want me to bring you something?"

"Yeah," Divinion said, looking from one of us to the next. "A couple of pieces."

"Okay, then." Lanah began collecting her things into her purse.

"Shouldn't one of us stay here to look after our things?" I asked when all four of us had moved to the aisle.

Divinion snorted. "Boy, how much you really think we have to lose?"

❁ ⚓ ❁

Once we were outside the train station, the afternoon felt like a familiar song: the chattering of the magpies, the midday cacophony of townspeople. Grocery trucks moved down the street as people yelled, bartered, and ran away from, towards, or through their hellos, goodbyes, and lives. It wasn't much different from the town we'd started in, and there was no newfound sense of freedom in being miles away. As I walked over peanut shells and gum wrappers and squinted at storefronts with faded signs and whitewash, I realized how much farther I still had to travel. Dogs barked. Babies cried. Some children played cowboys and Indians; others played with dusty marbles in the street, and still others balanced on tin can stilts to make themselves a little taller and more important.

Lanah had heard from family members who'd traveled north before of a small outdoor café at this stop, which specialized in cabbage, coleslaw, and the best catfish sandwiches and lemonade in the state.

"You just looked like you could use a civilized lunch," she said. We walked a couple of blocks through clouds of dust that hung low to the street, trying to collect as little of it as possible on our persons. The air shimmered with heat, yet Lanah moved as effortlessly as I imagined she would move through any world, ethereal yet confident, with a practiced gentility that seemed wholly natural, announcing her presence by the click of her small heels. I wondered if Lanah were really her name, or if she'd invented it for the movie star she wanted to be. Between one store selling quarter hats and another selling ironworks, there was the small restaurant with two tables out in front; Lanah chose the one with the most shade. I pulled out her chair and she sat down without comment as if that was a courtesy she expected and deserved.

She was excited by the large Coke machine on the porch; even though she didn't order any Coke, she said that a vending machine at a Black restaurant meant the food was good and they were doing well. She obviously valued success.

"This heat," she said, once again brandishing the elaborate Chinese fan from her purse. The waiter brought us tall glasses of lemonade, seeds and pulp dancing around thick ice cubes before settling to the bottom. "My cousin here would like a larger glass," Lanah told him. "And fill it to the brim, please." Before the waiter left, she added: "And bring two beers. Seems like the right type of afternoon for those, too."

"What kind of—"

"Anything cold. It's been a long journey." She smiled until the waiter walked away and then added, for my ears only: "I know it seems like a lot, but it's a shame not to ask for everything you want, isn't it? Divinion doesn't think women should drink beer, either. But he isn't here, is he?" She looked at me for some sign of collusion or protest but found neither.

"We aren't really cousins," I said.

"How do you know we aren't?"

"We went over this. Plus, any basic knowledge of—"

"Basic knowledge?" she repeated. "You do seem like someone who enjoys their basic knowledge of things." She took a sip from her lemonade, careful of the condensation dripping down the glass. "Look, I'm sure someone was in the shed somewhere, and then in the shed somewhere else, and all of a sudden look at us: cousins enjoying a beautiful lunch together."

Cars passed. There were a few tables inside from which diners watched Lanah, enthralled.

"I heard white folks come all the way over from Tennessee to eat here," she said.

Those magnificent hazel eyes gleamed in the sunlight.

As if trying to stave off the sloppy compliment I was forming in my mind, she then told me that she wanted better skin. She claimed that she was a "mutt" rather than "mulatto," gave her signature half-smile, and selected an amalgamation of ethnicities (Irish, French, Bengali) that seemed to fit her mood. I got the impression that this was not a new game for her. When I pressed her about Irish towns and French provinces, though, she admitted that all she knew was her father was dark, her mother white, and the confusion gave her a status she enjoyed.

"You, though," she said. "You have good skin. It's a gift. Good skin or good hair. Don't take either of those for granted."

The best thing you can be, Lanah tells me, is a Frenchman, because then, automatically, you're exotic, empowered, important, and someone else, far away. For a moment we watched the blur of silver-tinged grasses as watery clouds eased past. Aphids hopped from leaf to leaf. Sparrows danced near our feet, capturing pieces of grease-laden potato chips that had tumbled from the table edges to the ground. In the low brush of a nearby field, dragonflies hovered and dandelion seeds drifted.

"So the exotic would make you happy?" I asked.

Lanah shrugged. "Close enough." Once again she reached into her purse in search of a cigarette, then, remembering their absence, sighed in frustration. "But I'm with Divinion now, and no two people can be happy at the same time. My momma taught me that." As soon as the waiter had brought our lunch and walked away, she leaned in closer. "I'm leaving him," she said. "As soon as we reach New York City." She started to smile again, but her expression changed when I simply chewed my sandwich, unfazed and unsurprised. I think she expected my reaction to be more dramatic, but from what flashes of herself she'd allowed me to see, I was anything but shocked.

I swallowed. "Why?"

"Certainly you can tell that I'm no two-dresses-and-an-iron-stove type of woman. I'm going to Harlem first, where things are happening. Who knows, from there."

"When do you plan on telling Divinion this?"

"Divinion won't understand. No matter what he says or pretends, he's a Southern boy at heart. This place gets into some people and it fills them up and never leaves. Me?" She inhaled. "I want to smell the rest of this world, something more than dust and sweat or coal when a man is on top of me. I want to clear all this dirt off of me. Let the ocean air fill me instead."

"And after Harlem, off to France?" I asked.

Her smile returned. "Why do you care? You ask that like you plan to blackmail me or something."

"Maybe I will."

She swallowed a sliver of ice and smiled even wider. "You won't tell Divinion."

"What makes you so sure?"

"Because you don't like him."

"I barely know him."

"That doesn't keep you from not liking him. And you think this little bit of knowledge is going to hurt him somehow. So you'll keep it for now, tight in your gullet, ready to spit it out when you think it will be useful. Or you'll keep it because you think that just having it, having some private knowledge over him, hurts him even more. Or you'll keep it for luck. You probably have a lot of good luck charms."

I thought of my grandmother's quilt, tucked deep into my suitcase, still on the train. It was precious to me but not enough to anyone else that I feared it being stolen. People rarely understand what others leave behind.

"What makes you think I don't like Divinion?" I asked.

"I've been watching you this entire time, as much as you've been watching me. And I can tell instantly when two men don't like each other." She sipped her beer. "But you're also jealous of him." She gave me a smoldering look over the top of her glass, ignoring the waiter who approached us wiping his brow, and continued on. "Yes, part of you is jealous of him."

"Jealous."

"Oh, you'd never admit it." She placed her glass back on her napkin and wiped the dew between her fingertips. "As much as you hate him, you envy him."

I mustered a laugh. "So you say."

"I say." She sighed. "Don't do that. Don't deny it. You're bigger than that."

"I'm not a jealous person."

"That's probably true. But you're jealous of what he has."

"Which is?"

"Me."

I swallowed hard. "Ah. For now, you mean. Since you're leaving him."

"For now. But you're jealous that he's the man I'm with." She was enjoying this.

I did watch Divinion—less than I watched her, but I watched him. I stared. I wanted to figure out what type of man he was and what had brought him to this train this day, with Lanah on his arm. Was the journey truly Divinion's idea or was it Lanah's? Mostly, though, I watched his tie. Through scratches of light that would crawl across the train car, then disappear, I couldn't determine precisely what color it was, nor the pattern. It wasn't that I didn't have a name for it; I couldn't determine anything about it. I've been trying to find that color-or-pattern ever since.

In the end, she was right. It was a fascination I fought against and hated myself for, but it was there.

With her fangs in the jugular, Lanah couldn't resist biting. "Tell me, what would you do if you had me?"

"I've only known you for a day."

"But you know me."

"Barely."

"People aren't that complicated, really. If you pay attention, they tell you what they want you to know, and you can figure out the rest." She sighed. "Certainly a man like you doesn't lack imagination."

I changed the subject. "Do you and Divinion have any children?"

"That's a stupid question. Do you see any children with us?"

"I thought you might have sent them ahead, or left them behind. People do that sometimes." A bumblebee lit on the edge of my glass of lemonade but flew away before I had a chance to wave it off. Lanah was silent for awhile. I saw this as a chance to get the advantage, to be the mouse that had a chance to scurry away before the cat pounced again. "Have you and he discussed children?"

"Children slow you down. Like pets."

"But it must be particularly worthwhile with someone so...appealing." I smirked, then we both began laughing. "I'm sorry. That was clumsy."

"Do you have children?" she asked.

"No," I answered, perhaps a little too quickly.

"Then I assume we have the same opinion on the subject." I took a long drink from my lemonade to let her impression cement itself. "History slows you down, too. I'm one for looking forward." She squinted as she surveyed the street again. "The South is rancid, dying. Decay or travel: we leave it one way or the other. I'm one for going as far as I can as fast as I can."

"Then why not the other side of the world? Asia?"

"Maybe someday. For right now I want to be interesting, not a novelty. Hey, you should travel with me."

"As what? Entertainment?"

"Believe it or not, you're interesting." She dabbed her lips with her napkin. "And if you can turn around your melancholy, then maybe you'll be worth something." She motioned for the check. "Think about it. We have a few more hours to decide the rest of our lives."

❋ ⚓ ❋

On the way back to the station Lanah took my arm. From the porches of the white clapboard houses people stared at us as if we were important, and I felt exquisite simply through proximity. Bees floated from one low flower to the next, languid in the heat and the faded colors of the bright day.

"I want to buy a magazine," Lanah said.

"There's probably one in the corner store."

"Not one I'd be interested in."

She wasn't in any rush. I had to shorten my pace to walk so slowly beside her. While sucking on one of the remaining slices of sugared lemon from our drinks, Lanah told me about all the clouds I might have missed on the journey so far—the shapes and configurations and what each one resembled as it disappeared into the distance. She seemed to take joy in every inch of the South we left behind us, and once we were back at the station, while

Divinion, Carvall, and other travelers crowded around a radio to hear sports scores and the news of the day, she ignored them all and spoke to me solely—in a full voice, ignoring sideways glances from those straining to hear wispy sentences from a distant announcer. She talked more about her future and what she envisioned for herself. Every so often she touched my arm for emphasis.

I was hers. She had my full attention, and used it, and only once did she speak about her past again, about the alfalfa and mulberries on her grandfather's land. That land, that farm, and that history were miles in the opposite direction of where she was headed, and she seemed content to be expanding the distance even more despite her detached appreciation of past beauties. When she was finished with the lemon rind, she threw it to a colony of ants huddled on the floorboards, and they immediately swarmed as if it were ambrosia.

※ ⚓ ※

Back on the train I noticed that, unlike before, Carvall and Divinion weren't speaking to each other. Lanah didn't seem to care why; she simply handed a catfish sandwich over to Divinion, who tore into it. Carvall's haircut was nice, and Divinion looked at it with pride as he ate. I asked Carvall to change seats with me, in order to be closer to the window, to watch the clouds and keep attention away from how often I stole glances at Lanah or inhaled deeply to collect a moment of her perfume amidst the constant smell of ash and dust. Later that afternoon, I watched the horizon as a wide field of cotton approached; once upon us, it lasted for miles, a sea of white unbroken by any figure or frame, not a single picker making their daily sixty cents nor a machine to break the vast calm. It was how I'd always envisioned snow.

"Salt," I said, inadvertently aloud.

Divinion laughed. "Shit, the only Carolina salt I know is cotton."

Carvall shook his head. "Oh, there's salt all over Carolina, salt from tears and blood and the dead. It's in every riverbed and blade of grass."

"Why in tarnation would I want to see that?"

"Can't see it anywhere else."

"Man, you can see that everywhere."

"Not like this." Carvall began looking out the window as intently as I was. "The whole South ain't nothing but a scar with some salt on it."

But to me, regardless of what they said, the field was salt and sugar and snow reflecting up to heaven.

The clouds thinned as we traveled farther. Each of us again took turns sleeping through the jolts of the train and the heat, as if each of us felt responsible for the others' belongings and well-being. I stayed awake from pure excitement, thinking of a possible future with Lanah and hoping the train would pass the ocean or any waters deeper than I'd seen. I watched bars of sunlight—peach through a swift cloud, then again blistering white—cross the train car. Near my foot there was a bluebottle enjoying a crystal of sugar or salt, then a morsel of white bread Divinion had dropped from his sandwich. A couple of times I tried to step on it, but it would escape. Yet always return.

On my last attempt Divinion asked, before I even knew he was awake, "You trying to step on that fly?"

"Excuse me?"

"You trying to kill that fly?"

"I was just..."

"My daddy is great at killing flies. You should meet him. People think the secret to killing flies is speed. No, sir. You ain't gonna be faster than those flies. They can sense the change in the air around them and slip away. What you need to do, see, is ease up on them. Go slow. So slow that they see or feel you coming, but they don't see you as a threat. They think your shadow is just the night, and your hand something ready to pass them by. That's when you strike. That's how you kill flies."

He smiled at me as the train jolted into the next stop, which seemed to ease Lanah and Carvall awake. Divinion kissed Lanah on the forehead, which she casually accepted.

"We're almost there, honey," he told her.

"Not really," I said, seizing my chance to correct him. "We have a few more hours. We probably won't even get to DC until—"

"That's not what he's talking about," Lanah interrupted.

"DC? Who gives a shit about DC?" Divinion asked. We could hear another transistor radio on the platform, and everyone inside the car strained to listen to the broadcast, first Cuban rhythms, then some news story or baseball game: evidence that the world around us still existed so far north and so tall in the day.

"I heard you can get good Cuban food in DC," said Lanah.

"Cuban food? What you know about Cuban food?"

"You don't know what I know." There was fire in Lanah's reply, and all of us felt it.

"We may change cars there," said Carvall. "No more of this segregation."

"Man, this is America. There will always be segregation." Divinion shifted in the seat. "I'm keeping my Black ass right here. DC ain't no capital of mine."

"What did I tell you. Always scared." Lanah bowed her head.

"At the interchanges they have those smooth rocks, about the size of my thumb." After holding up his finger to demonstrate, Divinion flattened the morsel of white bread with his foot. "Those rocks are the perfect size to throw at people. Put it in a sling and kill someone like the story of David and Goliath."

"Oh, c'mon," Carvall said.

"You watch. There are plenty of ways to kill us. You watch."

Divinion glared at us. I looked away. Through the window opposite ours there were the ragged tents of those who picked the fields, some no doubt hoping to jump on one of the trains in the middle of the night, then to hold on with all of their strength until they reached what they thought freedom was supposed to be.

We left without them, the train lurching into the swelter beyond.

❋ ⚓ ❋

Farther along I watched the swaying of marigolds, then brown grass—shining golden at times in the late daylight— and tried to find a rhythm to the wind's movement. Far across the field there was a bottle tree, strewn with sculpted glass like what my grandmother would hand out in the middle of the night. I pressed my hand to the window hoping to see some of the reflections of green and brown glass in my palm, but I was too far away. Miles passed like empty breaths. Farther north there was a sky the color of late summer pale, then diluted blood, then roses, then flames.

In my daydreaming I lost part of Lanah and Divinion's conversation until it was directed towards Carvall and me.

"I'll tell you what, then," Divinion was saying. "Let's get off the train."

Carvall stared. "Get off the train."

"What I said. Let's get off the train."

Lanah stretched her slender fingers and turned to the window.

Divinion looked to me. "You and me, then."

"What?" I answered. I didn't want to let on how distant my mind was. "I'm not sure..."

Lanah's silence caught my attention as she focused intently on something beyond the window. Everything out there was far away. She bowed her head, as if whatever she had just witnessed was gone, or maybe just an illusion.

"Come on. Come meet my daddy," Divinion implored. "I can't travel all this way without saying hello. Come meet my family. They like new company." He flashed his brightest smile and, predicting my objection, added: "You're wearing a tie," as if it were the first time he'd noticed.

"But the train..."

"I know this stop. It's a long one. We've got three, four hours before we depart, right, honey?" He patted Lanah's leg. She didn't respond. "Besides, you can help me carry some food back for these two."

It was raining at the station when the train arrived; jagged streaks of tears across the windows cut into the soot. I watched a few droplets merge, then float away. I waited for thunder, but none came.

"When it rains I think it's my ancestors spitting down on me. I don't like going out in the rain," Divinion said. At first I thought he was rescinding his invitation. But by the time he and I stepped onto the platform, the rain had stopped, the cigarette-ash clouds had moved eastward, and everything stained dark by the storm seemed to dry instantly.

Black and white passengers wordlessly passed each other, as if each had a place and purpose, and in the humidity the station smelled like lye and old bleach: a place trying to be cleansed, or erased. As we approached a phone booth at the end of the station, Divinion took a nickel from his pocket, asked me for another, and simultaneously flipped each in the air, watching them spin before clenching them in his fists. He turned to me, arms outstretched, fists closed—searching my face, I'm still convinced, for fear or surprise or admiration of his parlor trick.

"Here's what we're going to do," he said as he turned his fists palms upward. "If both of these coins are on the same side, heads or tails, we drop them in that phone over there and call my brother-in-law to come pick us up. If they are on different sides, we walk."

I looked at the wall planks behind him, each a different faded color.

At that moment I realized how much he believed in luck and chance, the fluidity and power of each. Maybe that was his secret for attracting the type of woman I was already enchanted by: adventurous and bold, yet always weighing risk and reward. This journey to his family's home might provide some answers. In addition, I wondered if refusing Divinion's offer and staying on the train would arouse suspicions regarding my interest in Lanah. Maybe this was his test. Joining him, I reasoned, would solve two problems.

I looked at his fists, still hiding the coins. "Why are we choosing at all?"

"We aren't choosing. We're letting the Lord do it for us."

I waited. "Am I supposed to guess?"

"No, we just leave it up to Providence." His smile widened. "Deal?"

When I nodded, he opened his hands as if presenting me with a gift. Then he shoved the mismatched coins, and his hands, into his pockets and started walking up the road.

Before long, Divinion seemed even more exhausted by the walk than I; neither of us was wearing the right footwear for anything more than pacing up and down the length of a train car, and as we followed the road, avoiding the puddles that remained from the earlier shower, specks of mud collected on the tops of our shoes. We felt each stone beneath our soles.

Our shadows lengthened as we moved. Clouds of insects amassed over the fields and in perfect, hovering spheres alongside the cattails and sedges and dry ferns at the road's edges. Up ahead, beyond a line of trees, the road dipped into a valley flush with the smell of honey locusts and the call of distant birds. I could hear a river nearby—uncertain, thick waters rushing over stone, tumbling through the knotted roots of trees and emerging like claws.

"People say there are alligators and stray dogs out here," Divinion said, tipping the brim of his fedora as if to acknowledge each. "But I always say that if there's the first there surely can't be the second."

I looked back towards the station. "Are you sure Lanah didn't want to come with us?"

"My family can't stand Lanah. Never could." He wiped his brow. "I'm sure I don't have to tell you why."

I thought this was when he would slide into asking me what Lanah and I talked about at lunch, and that this was also my chance to punish her confidence in me and prove her wrong: prove I am worth something, something dangerous.

"She can come across the wrong way sometimes," he said. "It's just her way. My family has never liked it."

"She..."

"She's a good person," he continued. "But she can seem kind of uppity." He waited for me to reply, but I only stared at the road ahead of us. "Like Lanah thinks she has some family overseas. All she has is some postcard from her white grandmother with a faded stamp from some country she knows nothing about." He rubbed his shoulders. "She don't mean no harm, though. I want you to know that."

※ ⚓ ※

Above the tops of trees the sky was albumin, almost cellophane, which darkened the leaves against it to black. Although the sky was crisp, there was still moisture in the air. We heard bits of a voice yelling from a distance, and Divinion laughed.

I started to ask, "How much farther—"

"Ain't no rain!" he yelled back at the voice. "Took us no time at all!"

There was more yelling over the rustle of leaves and insects, and Divinion's pace quickened. He was home.

After a few more steps the road opened to an enormous meadow with a large colonial home, freshly painted, and thick orchards behind it, the trees perfectly aligned. This vision made me stop short, enraptured. It was so far from the hardscrabble world I'd envisioned as Divinion's past and assumed to be all of ours. The front lawn was perfectly emerald and manicured, tiny beige grasshoppers leaping from blade to blade as we approached. As we moved closer the house expanded in my vision, its alchemy only broken by the sounds of a few grey squirrels in the nearby oak trees.

"It's..." I began. I tried to find the words to tell Divinion how magnificent this was, but he was focused on capturing other words in the breeze. Once we were on the gravel pathway, a wide, oak-stained, porch opened before us, and after a short run up its three steps, Divinion wrapped his arms around someone whose face I couldn't see; the two of them laughed as they hugged and he spun her around. I lingered behind, inhaling everything I never thought possible.

"Fine, fine," Divinion was saying as I ascended the steps myself. Then I was met with names, new faces, and outstretched hands. Divinion leaned over a small figure in a rocking chair, draped in a shawl. "This here is Minister," he announced, almost proudly.

"Oh!" the older lady exclaimed. "You brought a minister by to see us!"

"No, Mama. His *name* is Minister," Divinion said.

The woman tried to not appear perplexed.

"Minister Peters," I replied to release the tension, as if my last name would offer some sort of explanation.

"Well, that just means you must be extra holy," she answered. Divinion laughed. "You hungry?"

Before I could finish saying "Yes, ma'am"—more from politeness than the need for nourishment—Divinion said: "Are you kidding? You should watch this boy eat," and then he was leading me through the rickety screen door and into a living room with high ceilings of dark oak. It appeared to be a plantation house reclaimed, filled with dark faces, the eyes of each person sparkling as they looked at me. Each smile was genuine, and each handshake welcomed me as if I were a prodigal son returning. I met aunts, uncles, cousins, nieces, nephews, matriarchs, patriarchs, and children with perfect white teeth who led me through the various rooms upstairs—some with well-made four-post beds that had beautifully embroidered quilts over clean linen—and pointed out the pictures, in gilded or silver frames, of those family members who weren't there. I looked for photographs of Lanah or a younger Divinion, but I was playfully whisked past them all so quickly that I couldn't recognize anyone.

In spite of the heat and humidity, everyone at the house was in their summer Sunday finest, and once back downstairs I was given what I was told was the most comfortable chair in the house, as dinner would be served shortly. Plastic carpet runners glistened. I watched a boy in spit-shined patent leather carry a small box turtle through the house, from the front yard to the back. A little girl asked me, the closest adult, if she could have a cookie, but by the time I'd looked around to see if anyone else could confirm the request, she was gone; I picked an abandoned pink ribbon from the floor and placed it on the nearest mantle. There were no clocks anywhere, no radios, and no telephone to which Divinion could have called from the station; nonetheless, this experience was well worth the money lost. Somewhere someone mentioned: "Oh, don't start him lying," and I heard Divinion's laugh; I smiled, too, even though I didn't know where Divinion was. I wondered how I would be received if I ever returned home again.

Stories and debates folded one upon the other into music, with tips of laughter as the syncopation. I blinked as everything around me sparkled, shimmered, then glowed. Light refracted from crystal doorknobs. An old man sat next to me and asked for my story, but for the life of me, for all that I was, right then I couldn't remember any of it.

A large ham emerged from the kitchen and dinner was served. I was invited to the head of the table but took the seat nearest to me at the moment instead. I was also asked to say grace.

"But he ain't no minister, Mama," Divinion said to the older woman at the head of the table. "I told you that."

"The man can still say grace, though, can't he?"

Before I could reply an older gentleman, who I assumed was Divinion's father, started. Heads bowed, and once he finished delivering the blessing like a coronation, children

73

were adjusted and handed their cutlery, then platters were passed counterclockwise.

Everything was clean, ivory, sugar, lead crystal, bone. White linen tablecloths and doilies and placemats and napkins and runners. Glasses of iced tea with lemon slices on the rim and lemon seeds at the bottom. As he ate, the old man at the head of the table had the calmest smile and the quietest eyes behind his glasses. Every bird outside sang. A light breeze caught the linen curtains every so often, bringing the songs of distant frogs with it. There were no houseflies, only a ladybug now and then, which would fly away as soon as the children noticed it and giggled. The adults laughed together as they passed Cornish hens and candied yams around the table, along with fried corn and fried okra, buttered carrots and peas, rolls and cornbread, mashed potatoes and potato salad, chicken baked or smothered, country rice with butter or salt or sugar, collards with smoked hamhocks alongside, a pot roast, oxtails in gravy. There was a calm in every sound and a silence in every movement. Everything, every morsel, cut easily. Every bite was seasoned and flavorful; nothing tasted hidden or false. It was as if this were where every incandescent pure thing in the world landed, softly. I tasted everything, asked for seconds to quiet my stomach for the rest of my journey, and thought to myself that this is what encompassing love, pure sunshine, must feel like.

After dinner I found my way to the bathroom—tile floors, exotic vials of perfumes on a small silver platter, hand towels with buttercups and wild flowers embroidered on them, a circular porcelain sink with a clawfoot porcelain bathtub behind it, a box of scrubbing powder well used, and the smell of rosewater and quicklime filling the room. I spent longer than expected washing my hands, cleaning the dirt from my shoes, washing my hands again, and staring at my reflection in the clean mirror. I nearly rubbed my knuckles raw. My face seemed unfamiliar, welcomed. I leaned in closer as if to memorize the striation in each eye. I then blinked, repositioned myself, and, once convinced I was who I thought, released the weight that seemed to hold my feet to the floor, willing them to carry me back to the hallway and the smell of pine oil on hardwood floors.

When I returned to the dining room, bowls of strawberries and sliced peaches, with slices of pound cake or coconut cake with cream frosting, were being passed, while the men in their light suits and the women in their breezy dresses settled into one chair or the next. Some of the children rested their heads in the newly available laps. I carefully closed the screen door behind me and stood on the open porch, almost as wide and deep as the house I'd left behind, watching fireflies emerge and introduce themselves to one another in the early evening. The vast green lawn, encircled by magnolia trees, had a birdbath to one side and a lone peacock strutting along the other. Behind me there was the smell of cinnamon and molasses. The air was sweet on my skin and tongue, and the fields of grass swayed deep green in one direction, pale mint in the other. I imagined swans and rabbits nearby. A dragonfly hovered near the railing, then flitted away. I inhaled and tried to hold it all in. I looked around for Divinion; in the grand waltz of everything, the other names failed me.

Still awake, unlike many of the other children, a little boy tugged at my shirt sleeve, then giggled when I turned to him and ran away. A teenage girl with caramel eyes came by and placed her hand on my shoulder before asking, "Will you be staying with us?"

I looked back at the fields and the twisted willow trees in the distance. I inhaled again, wanting to fill every cell of my lungs. "Is there an orchard somewhere?"

"In the back. You want to see it?"

I shook my head. I noticed another bottle tree, this one with a thick underbrush beneath it, speckled with wild spring flowers. Beyond that was a cypress tree, tall as a ship's mast, split by lightning, with two rain crows in the high branches. Beyond that, the remnants of a cast iron fence. Beyond that, a single gravestone, which had tilted as the earth settled. Beyond that, the tree of knowledge. I turned to look up the gravel road Divinion and I had walked earlier. "I have someplace to be."

"You going North?" she asked.

"There ain't nothing happening there that can't happen here too, good or bad," I heard an older woman—Mama?— say, and in her voice I could tell she really believed it; in the end I couldn't see the point in arguing.

Another young woman, lighter-skinned and presumably in her twenties, appeared. "Now, Mama, a lot is happening up North."

"A lot is happening everywhere, all of the time. Doesn't mean it's anything good."

A skinny man, lanky and in his thirties, appeared and handed Mama her glass of sweet tea, a napkin wrapped around it to absorb the condensation, then wrapped his arm around the young woman's waist. "Doesn't mean it's anything bad, neither. That's where Divinion is headed."

"Makes no sense," Mama declared. "You could go out west. Make something of yourself in Texas in the oil business. Wouldn't have to go so far."

"Texas is as bad as here, Mama," the young man protested.

"Besides," the young woman added, "Who would want to get their hands even blacker?"

The couple laughed; I smiled, and the young man introduced himself as Divinion's brother-in-law, Ryland. The young woman he held was Cynthia, his wife and Divinion's baby sister. I wanted to ask more about my travel companions but wasn't sure how close Divinion's ears were.

"You could go to California," the older woman continued. "I hear it's heavenly in California."

"I have an uncle in California," I lied. They waited for a moment, expecting me to add more, but that was all I could imagine, so I excused myself to look for Divinion.

I walked around the rest of the house, searching. Soon enough the train would be departing, leaving little time for us to return to the station. My heart felt light yet full. I circled the house three times, stepping over islands of children napping or happily playing with pencils and toy cars. I floated through the haze of sweet tobacco in the living room and the laughter of the women in the kitchen, their hands submerged in soapy water. I went back out on the porch, where I'd stood earlier, and made a declaration: "I can't find Divinion."

Ryland still had an arm around his wife. "Divinion left a while ago with a plate of food for Lanah."

"What?"

"He said you'd catch up." As he spoke, heat and panic quickly rose in me. "He said you'd keep track of time."

Time. The train seemed like a lifetime ago.

"He said you knew."

I managed some kind of smile, but inside I felt awkward, ridiculous, and rude, being unsure of the exact hour (there were no clocks in view). I was at least sure I had no time to say goodbye to everyone and properly thank them for their hospitality and magic. I felt shattered and foolish as I mumbled my thank-you's to the handful of people nearby. Down in the yard, bushes trembled in the early evening breeze, and as I stepped from the porch onto the gravel walkway, distracted, I stumbled and fell. The leaf-strewn earth flew up to meet me. When I arose, it was with the imprints of pebbles deep in my palms. I quickly brushed myself off, thinking about Lanah seeing me like this.

"You okay?" Ryland asked.

"Yes, I..." I knew the direction I needed to take, but the distance eluded me. Still, I started walking. The flawless sky above the trees had grown wispy with virga.

There was a flurry of whispers, then Ryland said, "Don't you worry, Minister, I can drive you to the platform where the Dawn Lightning is supposed to stop next. Cut right through. Not a problem at all."

This was followed by another round of whispers.

"He's our guest," Ryland insisted, louder. "We have to take care of him."

"Divinion didn't. Just left."

"Hush."

"Let C.C. come and get him," said Cynthia. I turned just in time to see her slip her hand into that of her husband as if to restrain him, or take hold for safety.

"C.C. ain't leaving his house this time of night. You know that."

She turned to me. "Why don't you just stay here for the evening? I'm sure my brother-in-law will watch your things, and you can meet up with him farther along."

"You are more than welcome to stay," the old woman agreed. "We have everything you need here."

I believed her. Every part of my soul wanted nothing more than that.

Ryland withdrew his hand from his wife's. "You two are being crazy. You're making this man think we're country and scared of our own shadows up here. Like we ain't got no sense."

"Now, Ryland."

"I'll be all right." He smiled at the both of them, then turned to me. "I'll get you to that train, and I'll be all right."

✳ ⚓ ✳

"You'll have to adjust the seat a little," Ryland said as I climbed into the passenger side of his beige Plymouth holding the plate of food I'd been given for the rest of my journey. "My wife—" he stopped short as if he were thinking of her for the first time in months, as if he already missed her. The smell of easy rain and cypress was in the air again, and through the windshield I looked for new stars in the sky, but none emerged. The trees beyond, twice as old as any of us, were still darker than the sky above. There was a metallic scrape as he turned the key, and the anemic engine shuddered as the car started. "There. We're on our way."

Ryland eased the car onto the dirt road Divinion and I had walked earlier, where night shadows now haunted the tossing branches of the trees. I looked in the rearview mirror as we pulled away from the house, but no one was waving. It was as if they all expected to see me again soon enough—or neither of us ever again.

The world thinned as we left the grounds. The air seemed like paper, easily torn, and the moon appeared on the horizon as Ryland's slim fingers tightened on the car's steering wheel. Everything about the Plymouth was thin: thin tires and a thin frame that rattled as Ryland struggled to avoid puddles, pits, and craters in the road. Each one we hit sent the car on a new trajectory that Ryland had to correct. At times we would pass beneath a canopy of trees and Spanish moss only to emerge amid expanses of empty pastures with abandoned farmhouses decaying in the distance. We crossed a stream with a garbled, spectral voice that seemed to flow in a westerly direction instead of east to the ocean, though I'm not sure what its final destination could have been. The headlights were little relief in the approaching darkness, which Ryland leaned into as we sped forward. The barking of loose hounds would approach us, then fall away. Ryland didn't look at me as I sat back in the passenger seat, watching the fields and the lacework juniper trees become shapes in the night. The darkened world seemed empty. There was static on the radio.

"We'll make it," Ryland finally said, as if to assure us both.

In that same middle distance, towards a ridge of small hills against the fading sun, there were the silhouettes: bodies swinging and decayed, heads with only spines connected, the shapes of all kinds of animals feeding. There was the smell I wish I didn't know: moss and burnt flesh, mixed with the scent of the remaining life rotting. I longed for the smell of my grandmother's quilt instead.

Ryland noticed me staring. "Don't look over there," he warned as he kept his eyes straight ahead. "There are ghosts over there."

"I've seen ghosts before," I lied.

"Not ghosts like those. Those ghosts follow you, climb into your soul and never leave." He leaned forward. "Don't catch their eyes."

I looked instead at the road before us, dimming still under the car's headlights. I gripped the dinner plate in my lap for greater balance. At points I expected the car to dip into quicksand, and for the both of us to safely disappear.

I'd seen a lynching before, along with the remains of one, pieces of flesh in the moist dirt, the body left ashen and charred as it dangled from the rope for all of us to see in the morning. From the shadows we watched the whole thing: the collecting pale crowd, the candy and lemonade vendors, the cousin proclaiming the man's innocence to the deaf torches and the steadfast indifference of car headlights, the man beaten and dragged to the tree while begging for his own life as well as the lives of his wife and children, the cheers as the rope was tied and tightened, the hood, stained with dried spit and rancid sweat, placed over the man's head, the man's struggles as the noose went around his thin neck, the further cheers as the rope was pulled taut, the way the man ascended into the air, at first holy and angelic, the way the man's body struggled for breath as white children played and asked their parents for popcorn and salt peanuts; the way the man's body twitched once fully suspended; the convulsions and spasms that continued when the body was set on fire, still alive, smoke and flames rising, the smell of ashes and sweet gale, the crowd losing interest and heading home as the corpse continued to burn, the mother rushing towards the body once the crowds left, wailing to the moonlight and the night birds, her cries for us to help her take the body down—as if there was a hope for life, life after all of that.

We'd heard of Black men skinned alive and left for the possums and stray dogs. We'd heard of mixed children thrown onto cinder piles or drowned in lakes moments after their first breaths. As children, we were told of plantation owners who crucified their slaves along a makeshift Appian Way, burning the corpses afterwards. Mass graves didn't surprise us. We believed in horror, and horrible men. Bad things happened, and in the morning we went on with our games: making handprints in the wet earth, hoping they would last through the entire afternoon or marveling at how long our fingers had grown.

I felt myself blink. I tried to move my mind elsewhere, and all of a sudden I was jolted by the memory of a cracked plate, different from the one I now held, at dinner—a small chip that I'd forgotten about until now. I wondered when the plate would be discarded without anyone thinking twice; I wondered why it was still there at all.

There was a single fat lantern in the lobby of the station, swaying as it illuminated the bare floorboards, sweeping light from one side of the station to the other. To me the place looked abandoned, but Ryland assured me that the Dawn Lightning would stop there. As the car slowed he shook my hand vigorously, as if we were brothers ourselves, as if he needed some sense of family right then. I thanked him and wished him luck, but I should have said more. I wanted to tell him to come with me, that it was safer, but I didn't know that for certain, or what our northern destination would really be like. I wanted to tell him to take me back to the house with him, that maybe two people in the car would prevent any others from approaching, that if he waited at the station until morning the danger would be gone, but the words soured on my tongue, then dissolved. I knew they weren't true.

I got out of the car. "Take care of Divinion, now," Ryland said, and before he pulled away he gave me the kindest smile I've ever seen, even to this day. I waved, and before I knew it the Plymouth had raced into the darkness of the thin trees beyond us, the red taillights like tiny shrinking eyes. Then headlights, like the great golden eyes of wolves, came alive in the darkness and veered away, following Ryland's beige sedan, bouncing away along the narrow road that had brought us here. For a moment I hoped that those lights would turn back, maybe come after me instead; I wanted that. They didn't. More lights joined the hunt. Eventually they all disappeared into the distance, and there were no sounds in the night, besides the wind.

I sat on the nearest bench and waited. Flies lit on the plate of food I was carrying, but because of the wax paper covering, they flew away, disappointed yet alive. On the floor beside me there was a crust of bread with butter, a mother layer of mold forming along the edges, a fat caterpillar inching towards it. Across from the station stood a large tree I couldn't recognize, bark falling away from its side, leaves glistening in the new moonlight as if they were wet, bursts of seeds glowing silver on the tips of the branches. Every other second there was a rustle of wind, but nothing appeared. No tufts or leaves fell. Those were the only ghosts, I told myself.

❋ ✝ ❋

In the nighttime shadows aboard the Dawn Lightning, I wasn't sure if Lanah smiled at my return. Trails of moonlight flickered through the windows. My seat was still empty, waiting, with both Lanah and Divinion laughing at something Carvall must have said, although he wasn't laughing himself.

"You made it!" Divinion announced with enthusiasm. I wondered if he was wearing a different tie.

"Your brother-in-law gave me a ride," I said as I returned to my seat next to Carvall, who said nothing, and Lanah, who—I could tell now—did give the slightest smile after all. I placed the plate of food in Carvall's lap, which he accepted without breaking his gaze toward Divinion.

"Of course he did," Divinion proclaimed with a confidence that bothered me. "You're family now."

"I hope he'll be all right. After he dropped me off there were these cars..." I began.

"I helped him buy that Plymouth back in '43," Divinion said.

I tried again. "There were other cars..."

"He'll be fine. Always is," Divinion said.

I settled into my seat. Something told me not to believe whatever he said next; as he started into his story about how he'd loaned Ryland the money, I closed my eyes and let the evening pass into night, clutching my belongings tighter all the while, protecting what little I thought was still mine. In the new darkness the train had a rhythmic clatter that lulled the mind into its own silence. There was a slight drizzle outside, so I found syncopation in the rain-drops and fell into a deep sleep that seemed like drowning. I saw myself sinking farther and farther into the darkness, my arms and legs above me as I descended without air or relief, all of which I found calming. I prayed that this was how my daughter had felt on her descent. Later, I could hear Lanah and Divinion whispering in the distance, but in order to make out the words I would have had to ascend from the calm in which I found myself, and right then the effort hardly seemed worth it.

※ ⚜ ※

Then there came a harsher whisper in the night, and as I came awake, head slumped, my gaze fell on the empty dinner plate, where flies now collected on the morsels and gristle that remained; I couldn't tell if the plate were cracked at all. When I raised my head I saw Carvall muttering, staring straight ahead at Divinion. At first I thought I was a trespasser into their late-night conversation, but Divinion was fast asleep; still, Carvall stared at him with an intensity usually reserved for violence. I'd seen eyes like that before. I thought about interjecting, but from the change in my breathing Carvall must have noticed that I was awake. His eyes met mine for a second, and I crafted a quick smile.

"The food was good, wasn't it?" I said. "Divinion's family was very—"

Carvall interrupted. "What does he know, huh?"

"I'm not sure I..."

Carvall jerked his head at Divinion. "What does he know?"

I looked over. "I'm not sure."

"Thinks he knows so much about everything. He don't know shit." I let Carvall pause for as long as he needed. "I can't stand niggas like that. No good, no account..."

"His brother-in-law..."

"I wanted to stop the train for you. Tell the porters to slow a minute, give you some time. You walking alone? The crazy white folks in that country? I would have stopped the train for you." He lifted his smallest finger so slightly and pointed it at Divinion. "But he said it wouldn't do no good. That no white conductor was going to stop no train for a nigga, any nigga. But I would have tried." He paused again.

"Niggas like him. They never try. They'd let us all drown so they can sniggle and tell stories about it later."

"I think..."

"I can tell you ain't like that." I wanted to ask how. "You and me, we're cut different. But look at him. Got his little cotton-and-corn money and now he thinks that makes him something. He'll learn. A thousand niggas just like him."

I waited a moment. "His family thinks..."

"Ain't nobody touch your stuff, though. I made sure of that. I told them: 'He'll be back. He'll make it.'"

I wanted to ask what stories Divinion had told about me while I was away. Maybe he'd told them that I wanted to stay behind. Maybe that I would be happier there, without them. Maybe that they, and the entire group heading north, would be better off without me. Maybe that I'd metamorphosed into something else during that dinner—something beautiful, perhaps, or frightening. I wondered how they saw me now.

"They left me there, too," Carvall said.

"What do you mean?"

"In the war I was with a whole bunch of niggas like that—one of the only fighting forces, but still a bunch of niggas. We were ambushed one afternoon in this thick, black forest with these thin trees, and cold everywhere. The shooting started before I could even see anything, just splinters and ice and then I felt this warmth and wetness in my side. Then the pain hit, and I was on my knees before I knew it. I heard more bullets, screams, shattering.

I fired a few times at these German soldiers—just pale, gangly German children running towards us, so small in the trees' shadows—and I'm sure I killed a few of them, and I didn't care. The whole war was white people killing other white people but there we were. Then I remember this cold feeling spreading through me, with my fists pushing through the frost on the ground until the dirt beneath wrapped around my fingers. Then I was falling forward. Then nothing."

Carvall held his breath for a while, as if easing the memory upward through his throat. "I can remember a few more screams, then silence, and when I opened my eyes I saw a few of my company walking away, some wounded, but walking. I reached out." He took a long breath. "I reached out, cried out to them, and those niggas. Those niggas looked at me for a minute and then turned away as if they couldn't be bothered to help me. As if I were worse than the enemy. As if I were nothing at all to them. No brother. No friend. Not even a man. Just dirt. Nothing at all." I thought of asking whether he was sure they truly saw him and knew he was alive, but this was Carvall's truth; who was I to pry it away from him? He swallowed. "We should all be something to someone, whoever we are. I believe that."

I watched the tension in his body release and then slowly return as he spoke again. "When I woke up the second time it was night. Quiet. I turned myself over and saw these big holes in the sky, between the clouds, where there were no stars at all. No moon. I heard no footsteps. No one else breathing. I was scared to breathe myself, but I took in this big gasp of air and nothing happened. No voices. I was all alone." He swallowed again. "They left me. My friends and fellow soldiers. They left me there like the other corpses. Those niggas..."

This time he squinted even closer at Divinion. "Laughing at me. Back at the barracks drinking cheap wine and laughing at me. And I wanted them all dead. Black and white. I wanted every Kraut and every yellow man to kill all of them, then each other. I wanted to yell and cry out but I wasn't sure who else was around. I wanted to stand up but I was too scared to move. So I stayed like that the rest of the night, and the next morning I rose to my knees and looked around. Some of my friends were there—dead, eyes staring in all directions, haunting me to this day—and German boys as well, some of them almost ten years younger than we were. There was still a ringing in my ears, and I tried to stand, pressing my hand against the closest tree for balance, but that pain in my side returned and I dropped to my knees again, then my back, watching that clear sky."

At this Carvall bowed his head, wiped his brow, and then stayed so still for a while that I thought he'd fallen asleep, but eventually he went on. "I watched it turn to night again, but I wasn't dead. I crawled a bit to steal a canteen of water from one dead man, a crust of bread from the satchel of another, but I always returned to the place I'd been shot, the place my blood collected, to rest. Like I'd left my soul there and I had to return to it. I slept there, cold, for another night. Waiting."

He squinted as if fighting against tears that would burn should they reach his skin. "Waiting to die. Waiting for someone. I was waiting in the grass and frost and dirt, with all of those rotting bodies. In the mud I couldn't tell what was water and what was blood. What was my own spit, blood, the water around me. Everything tasted like salt. And then I just started yelling because I wanted to hear my own voice, because I didn't care anymore if I lived or died. I wanted someone to either save me or kill me and I didn't care which. I yelled in English and in what little German I knew. I yelled for hours until my voice gave way. Then I started crying until I drifted away again."

I could tell that returning to that moment was what he'd feared most when starting this story—not the bullets or the betrayal, but the moment when he decided on suicide rather than a future, or more pain.

Here, on this train, we were safe. There was no dirt. There was no time. No one was leaving or pursuing or waiting for us. But I'm not sure how much of a comfort that was.

Because his eyes glistened in the moonlight, as if straining not to close again for fear of sleep, and so the story he carried could keep him awake and alive a little longer. "Lucky for me an artillery regiment came through the next day and picked me up. A white artillery regiment. A bunch of white boys saved me. I'm not sure how they even knew, but in the early morning I felt a boot against my side. I flinched, then I heard someone standing close to me yell that this one was still alive. I stayed with that troop a little while, about a day or two, until they dropped me off because they told me I wasn't good enough to stay with them. I wasn't good enough." He patted his coat pocket. "They gave me this here gun and pointed me in the direction of the nearest base and told me I'd better run or they'd shoot me themselves." The moon reflected the tears that balanced in his eyes. "So I ran. I had a bullet festering in my side but I ran and they laughed until I turned a corner and they couldn't see me anymore. A few hours later I made it to that base, then they sent me home. And I never saw that troop or those niggas again. And ain't nobody call me a hero. Not a single person, Black or white. Then again, I didn't do anything special. All I did was survive. Seems like that's all we ever do."

"Sometimes that's enough," I said.

"But for what?" He stared at Divinion even harder than before. "For who? For niggas like these?"

And before I could respond, and with a quickness I'd never seen in him until then, he pulled his Army revolver from his coat, pointed it at Divinion's forehead, and pulled back the hammer. I froze, feeling every shift of the train against the tracks. I wondered why he'd been carrying it like that this entire time. What else was he afraid of on this journey? I didn't ask. I glanced around, but no one else seemed to see what I was seeing—or, if they did, they figured it wasn't their affair and pretended to be asleep, not willing to interrupt their own journeys for the fate of a stranger. Except for the eyes of the little boy, the one I'd seen when I first boarded the train. We stared at each other as I waited for the sound of the gunshot. When I turned back, the barrel of the pistol was touching the center of Divinion's forehead. Carvall exhaled, and to my surprise he shifted the aim to Lanah's cheek instead.

"Niggas like these. What good are either of them?" His arm was steady, the gun still cocked, and as the train shifted again, his finger did, too, a slow squeeze bringing the trigger a hair closer to firing.

Then, still calm, he removed his finger from the trigger and decocked the hammer. "Hold this for me," he said, and handed me the pistol.

I'd never held a handgun before. It was heavier than I thought it would be—an ominous weight, solid in spite of moving parts and chambers, with a finality to it—but I transferred it to my jacket pocket before anyone else could see.

I remember my father once took me up to the mountains to learn how to hunt. We wore our workday clothes, even though it got colder and colder the higher we ascended, frost sprinkling the low branches of the trees. I carried the rifle—one of the better models we sold at the store—cradling it under my arm, as I'd seen people do. When we came across a deer feeding, I pulled the gun from the burlap and handed it to my father, who handed it back to me. He told me to aim, stay quiet and steady, empty my lungs, then my thoughts, and fire. Which I did, grazing the animal in its side as it bolted away. We followed to where it had fallen in the chill mud and ice; it was still breathing, puffs of steam matching ours. My father told me to fire again, to finish it, if only for mercy, but I couldn't do it. The animal and I stared at each other, the cold wind cutting through our eyelashes, until my father took the gun from me and fired the last shot himself.

Carvall and I found nothing else to say to each other as the night sky cleared and the moon rose to meet our reflections. I expected Carvall to write more letters, scratching pencil against paper late into the night, but he didn't; he only stared. We avoided each other's eyes now, distant yet knowing, like brothers more than cousins; neither words nor names were important any longer. In the glass I watched his reflection slowly fall asleep to the rhythm of the train's movement. I wanted to ask if the midnight confession was the result of something that happened during my absence from the train earlier that night or of something that had transpired between him and Divinion, when the two of them went to the barber shop together. But I suspected it wasn't just one thing, one argument, one statement, one slight, one memory, one word. We're human beings. It rarely is one thing.

I thought of my uncle and how long he was alone in the West. I thought of each of his mornings by himself. I wondered how often he thought of my father and what he dreamed our life had become. I wondered if he could be visiting my father's grave right then. I wondered if, through all the cold nights and lonely meals, he'd ever found the respect and home that he was searching for when he left the island.

I touched my daughter's picture, still folded in my breast pocket. I remembered my grandmother's quilt, pulled it from the bottom of my suitcase, and wrapped it around myself for comfort as I tried to drift off to sleep. But a little while later I heard Lanah yawn, and she smiled when her eyes met mine in the darkness. I wondered if she was expecting an answer about whether I would travel with her. I didn't know how to tell her how close she'd just come to being murdered.

"I dreamt it was morning already," she murmured.

"What did the new world look like?"

She shrugged. "New."

Not wanting to stare, I glanced back out the film-coated window. "We still have a while."

"I wish we could see more stars from here. They are the most perfect little things where I come from. Like crystals dripping from the sky."

"My grandmother used to say there was no such thing as stars," I said. "Just holes in heaven where angels fell through."

"Hm. There we go again, thinking beautiful things need to fall." She looked down and twirled her wedding ring.

"Listen, I have to apologize for my husband leaving you with his family like that."

The term "my husband" jolted me and put me on the defensive. "I enjoyed my time there."

"They're simple."

"They are very nice."

"They're nice because they're simple. That's all they can be. That's all they'll ever be." She clasped her fingers and stretched her arms above her head. "Black people have to move beyond being nice all of the damn time. That's half our problem."

"And the other half?"

"It's too short of a train ride to get into." She rested her head on her husband's shoulder, a sign of ownership and triumph. "I'm just glad I pulled Divinion away from all of that."

"He's quite fortunate to have you."

"Make fun, but I'm telling you: being too yes-um to everybody is our biggest problem. History will prove me right."

"History."

"Shit, you aren't just another one of those Negroes scared of ghosts, are you?"

"I've been living with ghosts my entire life."

She looked around at the people and the baggage that strewed the car. "And look at this graveyard of old shit you're in now. Sorry."

Then, with the same confidence Divinion always showed

in having made a final proclamation—I wondered which of them had gotten that mannerism from the other—she closed her eyes and drifted back to sleep.

※ ☦ ※

County after county drifted by, but the moonlit landscape never changed—as if we were hovering. In the quiet, with everyone around me sleeping and all the planets higher in the night sky, I heard the rattle of my lunch tin beneath me and opened it once more. I wasn't hungry, but I scraped up a few morsels of the dried cornbread from the linen napkin, now translucent with dried grease, and dissolved them on my tongue. I tried to remember where I had kept this napkin in my kitchen. The drawer? A cupboard? Was it something my wife had purchased, or had I?

Now, though, it was just a piece of soiled cloth. I crumpled it and stuck it back in the empty tin, which I closed with a snap that rang through the train car. Still, no one stirred.

I picked up the tin and meandered towards the back of the train, lightly stepping over bodies—children stretched out in the aisles, each clutching their most prized possession as tightly as they could. A breeze washed in as I slid the coach door open, but none of the bodies stirred. I made my way to the next car, then the next, and the next, and as I crossed through each I didn't see strangers, neither Black nor white, simply contours I'd seen everywhere before, common silhouettes. None of the passengers seemed unfamiliar—or unlovable, regardless of how the years and sun had hardened their faces. These travelers were tempo-rary family. There was comfort in their snores and whis-tles and shifts and sweat. I stepped over them as silently as I could, moving past white faces who didn't bother to stop me and porters who didn't question what I wanted or where I was headed. When I reached the final door, I opened it too and let the wind rush past me. I watched the train tracks slipping away and merging to a point in the distance, while ever-new shadows of trees and hay rose and then dwindled and vanished.

I opened the lunch tin once more. The napkin stirred and billowed until the tin couldn't hold it any longer. When it reached the top it escaped into the air, danced on the wind, and flew beyond my grasp. I had to squint to see it light upon a yellow flower, then lift and float anew into the clear dark.

I thought of my grandmother and loss. Then I let the tin slip from my hands. It bounced onto the wooden slats between the tracks, end over end, as though running away. Then it stopped, and we kept moving. As I turned to go back to my seat, the wind caught my grandmother's quilt and tore it from my shoulders. I grabbed for it frantically, but soon it was beyond my reach as well—blowing along the tracks, into the distance, draping the past.

It was hotter than I'd thought it would be this far north or this late in the night, with the tang of soot and metal thick on the breeze. In the field beyond the train, a white tent glowed, illuminating wildflowers and clouds of gnats; I could hear shouts and drums and organs as the revival played into the moonlight. The preacher was a growl into metal and ether, and the tent—now a temple, the dirt beneath it consecrated and sanctified by the faithful—shook with bodies convulsing, swaying, and saved. There was singing and the screams of those moved by God—some like pain, some like ecstasy—as the pearl canvas rippled against glowing grass. I thought about all I was leaving, the tiny shards and slivers and jetsam of myself far behind along the tracks. Though the worshippers were obscured by the radiant tent, I saw each one of their faces, like those in the train, and thought I knew them all.

I returned to my seat and waited for the rest of the car to stir, leaving everyone unaware that the train was now a little lighter, a little faster, and a little closer to our destiny than they imagined, now that the weight of my history was behind us. For all the bodies surrounding me, their breathing constant in my ears, I felt alone. The children were quiet, and few babies cried. From time to time conversations bloomed, but whatever tatters I could catch sounded scratched, broken, less than whispers.

✻ ☨ ✻

Late-night stops were few. As long as the train stayed in motion, the night air through the open windows kept it cool; whenever it stopped, humidity blanketed us instead. I don't know what time it was when I woke to that dampness and the porters and engineers once again walking alongside the train, this time carrying lanterns and grimacing.

Jolted awake, Divinion whipped his head back and forth. "Yeah, this is the spot. This is the place." He pointed to a lone telephone pole in the distance that glowed with auburn light. "Look, there's that crooked telephone pole the man was telling us about."

"You know how many crooked poles there are in—" Carvall began.

Divinion interrupted. "Nah, I can feel it. We've got to be in Virginia. I can smell it in the night dew."

"You're crazy."

"Damn right I am. But this is the stop. I can hear the music from here."

I could not hear music or sense whatever tiny vibrations he seemed attuned to in the festering air. From the looks of it, Carvall couldn't either.

"We have to go," said Divinion.

"We don't have to go anywhere," replied Carvall.

"We promised the man. You sat right there in that barber's chair and told him—"

"I know what I told him."

"Well, c'mon, then."

"Even when I said it I had no intention of going."

"So you lied, then. You lied to that old man."

"I didn't lie to anybody."

"Then let's go."

"There isn't time."

"That old man said we'd have hours."

"What does some old man remember?"

Divinion pointed to the engineers outside. "Look at them milling around."

"So?"

"Besides, how much time do we need? This is our chance to cut loose."

"I don't want to cut loose."

"Bullshit. The hell you don't. You been cooped up in that uniform for how long now. I bet that tie is practically choking you."

"I'm fine."

"And before then you was cooped up in those barracks overseas."

Carvall cut him a glance I'd only seen when Divinion was sleeping, when he pressed the barrel of his gun against Divinion's cranium, then below Lanah's fluttering eyelid. "You don't know anything about me."

"I know you've got no idea what it's going to be like, and no idea what you'll probably be doing when you get up north, so why not have some fun now, boy?" Divinion shifted in his seat, impatient. "Minister wants to go."

"What?" I said.

"He does not," said Carvall.

"Sure he does. We're family now."

"Go where?" I asked.

"Nowhere," said Carvall with a finality meant to stop further conversation.

Divinion wasn't giving up so easily. "While we were in that barber shop this morning, this old man told us about this seriously jumping juke joint in the Virginia woods that we have to go to." He pointed. "Behind all that dried grass, right through those mangled trees, was the best greasy juke joint he'd ever been in. Said he danced and drank and hollered there until his feet bled, his knees buckled, and his throat was sore from whooping and moonshine. Best time he ever had in his life. Didn't he say that? Time of his life, boy." I no longer trusted the big grin that spread across his face. He seemed just as excited about this place as he had about seeing his family again—the family he abandoned me with. Sensing my apprehension, he added: "We don't have to stay long. A drink. Maybe a card game or two."

"I don't play cards." When had he ever seen me play cards? Who did he think I was?

He tried again. "The man also said there was plenty of nice women there."

"He didn't say 'nice'."

"No, he did not." At this Divinion burst into laughter again. I started to wonder if he was simply the type of person who got excited about things. Maybe that was what had appealed to Lanah so much about him, that perceived adventurousness made him affable until you got to know him better. Still—Lanah was at his side, not mine.

It was almost as if he sensed my interest there, too. "Maybe you'll even find a Lanah of your own." He kissed her on the cheek. "This one's taken."

"Do you want to go?" I asked Lanah.

"And deal with a bunch of drunk fools?" She didn't bother looking at either of us, though Divinion laughed at her question. "No thank you, doesn't sound like a place for me. I'll stay here."

"Yeah, you better stay here," said Divinion. "Doesn't sound like the type of place for a lady. My lady." He winked at me and flashed a smile of camaraderie that I'd never seen before, like he thought we were true brothers.

"Besides," Lanah continued. "I'm sick of chasing and babysitting Black men trying to figure out who they are and where they stand in this world."

"Now, that's got nothing to do with it," Divinion said. "Brothers got to have a little fun every once in a while, right?"

She unwrapped another golden piece of candy from her purse and placed it onto her tongue. As she noticed me watching she offered me a piece—which I refused, then immediately feared that refusing this small confectionary would be interpreted as rejecting the invitation to travel on with her. I wanted to accept her offer right there—*How many seas do you think we could cross together?*—but reasoned to myself that if I went to the juke joint, I could actually prove I was not the ball of sadness she claimed I was. I could prove that I was all Divinion was and more.

Also, I didn't know what would happen if Carvall and Divinion were alone together for that long—nor which outcome would be best for me.

"I'll go," I said. Once the words left my lips, it felt as if a hush came across the entire coach. Carvall and Divinion both stared. "I'll go," I repeated.

"There you go, Minister." Divinion slapped Carvall on the knee. "You heard the man."

Divinion rose to his feet. Still staring at me, Carvall rose as well, as if to confront him, but Divinion took it as compliance. I was the last to stand. Lanah didn't look up from beneath her hat at any of us.

"We'll be back," I said. "I promise." She didn't react, right when I needed her to. *We'll be together then.* I still wonder if I ever actually added those words, if they ever reached my lips from my mind.

It was just up the road, Divinion promised us every so often, a few yards more and two bends on. There were no streetlights, only a clouded moon and fireflies illuminating the marshes on either side of the dirt road. The sky seemed the color of ripe plums. Frogs and crickets silenced as we passed.

"Crocodile," Carvall said as he pointed to one of the swamps. Its surface crinkled under the mist and breeze, but I didn't see anything except mud, broken reeds, and tiny ripples from bass or salamanders already submerged, disappeared. I looked for snapping turtles. I looked for my reflection in the water. In the pitch lowlands and wet air I thought I saw the eyes of a possum, or maybe a boar, scurrying to hide its scent and itself. In places the murky waters had receded from their banks, leaving bare tree roots like tendrils or arteries. Further out in the waters appeared the silhouettes of two children, a boy and a girl, holding hands—but as I passed by, gaping, I recognized them as simple tree trunks. Not ghosts, not observers or judges or the abandoned or the lost.

The moon hid and shone, hid and shone, as high breezes swept the clouds across it. I wanted to see a comet or an eclipse, anything to let me know if God were still up there. Was Lanah or Ronalda looking at the same tattered sky?

The dirt of the road—slick, but not wet—now seemed to soften, which made Divinion walk even faster in excitement. As we approached, the place we were heading was more heat than light; we felt it long before we saw it. The rumble of horns, rhythm, and slide guitar. We felt the vibrations through our shoes, into our bones. Every other creature around us was silent, frozen, as if in the sights of a predator.

Then there was laughter, with scraps of conversation on the wind. Around the next bend headlights approached us, then the car turned onto a side road I hadn't noticed before. The music became louder with each step we took, and the headlights more frequent; we left the dangers of the road and walked through the tall, dry grass instead. Carvall looked back as if concerned about how far we'd come, and how we'd get back to the train later.

The closer we got, the more the shack revealed itself to be an old barn rigged with lights in full glow against the night, with patrons leaning against dilapidated farm equipment outside, and two hounds standing nearby—one scratching at something swallowed by the earth, the other keeping watch. Divinion nodded and tipped his hat to everyone he saw. He appeared just as much at home here as at his family's house, now miles away. Maybe he was more capable than I gave him credit for. With a few well-placed utterances of "ladies" and "my man," he deftly navigated through the crowd that loitered in the parking lot clad in zoot suits and A-line dresses. Up close the barn's paint looked faded, the siding warped. In the dimness of the car lights, the makeshift lanterns, the bare light bulbs, and the moon, I couldn't tell what color the building would be in the daytime. Beyond it there was no horizon, no stars. A few clouds lit with purplish underglow slid across the moon and then, like the rest of the world, faded away.

Divinion climbed the creaky, unbalanced planks of the entrance steps, where he leaned towards a fat man sitting on a stool and whispered into his ear, then slipped a few dollars into his hand. The man took a long drag from his cigarette and nodded. Divinion turned back to Carvall and me.

"Are we good?" he asked.

"We're good," Carvall said, more quickly than I'd expected.

My agreement wasn't needed. Divinion crowed over our heads into the darkness, as if he'd won.

❀ ⚚ ❀

Inside, the entire place radiated whiskey and heat. Women laughed without reservation. Men smiled with a comfort and ease I'd rarely seen on Black faces in the outside world. Young girls stood against the walls, tapping their feet, snapping their fingers, and singing along, in preparation for being asked to dance. Young men sat in the rafters, clutching the only beers they could afford and howling as amps blared feedback from the guitars and the singer screamed down a microphone, into the static. Below their dangling feet, the dance floor was packed and fluid. As slippery as each dancer appeared, they all seemed to move as one, anticipating the music—as if this were familiar to each of them, the place they truly felt home. They were connected, the music pulsing through them, wet. Fingertips brushed hips, then slid away. Clothing stuck to warm skin in some places but flared away in others. It was a long kiss between everyone in the room: sensual, passionate. Few of the dancers looked at their partners; most watched the floor as if waiting, through the vibrations, for something to arise.

The floorboards groaned and snapped in syncopation as fingers sliced across ivory and ebony keys. Cutting every sight were glints of brass and honey. Clear and golden liquors poured, then swirled in jars and glasses, some a translucent auburn like burnt stars, like all of us. Auric horns and trumpets growled and screamed into the thick night air. There were gold-plated rings and earrings and teeth and tie clips and tassels. Everyone and everything gleamed—from the chipped ice to the congolene—but not like the house of Divinion's family or the revival tent I'd seen earlier. This was the other side of things.

And we were in it, waves and cymbals crashing, every particle vibrating from the percussion. Divinion was alive. I tried to keep my eye on him in case he tried to leave me again, this time with no prospects for getting back to the station. Carvall, too, seemed cautious—if not of Divinion, then of our general safety. His gaze flicked around as if he were expecting something to leap out, ambush him, and make him betray the promise he'd made to himself over-seas, to never be vulnerable again.

Then we were lost—Carvall, Divinion, and I—separated into the crowd as if by an unseen whirlpool. Divinion let the swirling crowd take him; Carvall used a combination of skill, elegance, and determination to reach the bar, while I tried to manuever myself towards an empty spot near a wall beside the stage. I stepped over islands of tobacco spit-tle and dirt and foam, hoping to keep what balance I could in the storm. It wasn't dancing; it was celestial navigation. As I turned, I thought I saw Ronalda in the shadows and half-light, but it wasn't her, my spinning mind convinced me, only ghosts and steam and cigarette smoke. Like earlier that day, amid the ceaseless motion and the haze, I lost my footing and myself, unsure where to shift or bend or how, and I slammed hard into a smaller man. His hat was knocked askew by the collision, revealing a mass of oiled hair glistening beneath.

"Muthafucka!" I heard him say through the throbbing air. He grabbed my shoulder and spun me around, his dark skin slick, his eyes bloodshot and damaged. A pool of red in the right eye reached from the sclera to the caruncle.

A tall man stood behind him, a hat shadowing his eyes, silent.

"Oscar?" I muttered—not because he looked like Oscar Wheatts, only because he reminded me of someone missing.

"What?"

I mumbled an apology, trying not to make a scene, but when I turned away the man spun me around again, this time pushing his face within an inch of mine as he yelled, "Nigga, you got something to say?!"

"No!" I yelled back, perhaps erroneously interpreting his ask as a challenge rather than a request to repeat myself. Before I had a chance to clarify or explain, I saw Carvall's hand on the man's shoulder.

But as quickly as it was placed it was brushed away, and less than a second after that Carvall was sliding on the oily wooden planks beneath us. I wasn't even sure if he'd been punched—all I saw was that now he was on the ground and away from me. There was more yelling, barely audible above the music, and soon the mass of legs and rhythmic bodies engulfed him and he was hidden. The man with the red eyes was still in my face, his tall friend still silent behind him.

Although I couldn't make out a word he was saying, I knew that Red Eyes was screaming at me, spittle flying. A blue vein on his forehead pulsed, grew, the river of blood within nearly visible. At times he would pause, and his smile, his tongue, his gums, the inside of his cheeks, even the puffs of his breath gleamed red in the light. Then words rushed from him again, but still I couldn't hear over the music, or understand.

I stepped back, my heart pounding. The words kept hurtling towards me, faster and faster. I looked for Divinion. I looked for Carvall on the floor. The music kept playing while a small circle formed around us—a new song in the pulsating darkness—and I could no longer tell which limbs belonged to whom. I wondered if Carvall were bleeding. Divinion was gone. Again? Back to the train? Inside the music? Drowned? We were brothers. We were supposed to be there for each other. Everything was falling but nothing ever hit ground. I wanted to reach for my daughter's picture, but before I knew it the gun was in my hand instead.

For all its weight, the trigger was the softest thing I'd ever felt. The hard, sharp crack that rang in the atmosphere afterwards surprised me and everyone around me. All sound evaporated. The music stopped. Conversations ended. The smell of gunpowder mixed with the acrid air. I could hear ice melting and the seas falling silent.

❋ ⚓ ❋

There are moments in life when God has nothing to say to us, when there is a deafening silence surrounding our souls, when our lungs squeeze and eardrums still, when there is no air left to move through. I watched sweat pool against the dark opening in the man's forehead, collect, then stream down his cheek stained red. His eyes shimmered. I remember him blinking, just once, as I kept the gun pointed at his forehead.

Then everything about the light in him fell.

The tall man said and did nothing.

I wanted to see Divinion or Carvall in my periphery, or reflected in his eyes, but all was empty. My fingers and palms were damp from sweat, and my arm twitched as I held the gun steady. I spotted Carvall on the ground next to me, his breathing ragged; it was the only music that played. Had he been so close the entire time? His palms were pressed into the floorboards; his fingers were outstretched, reaching towards the heel of my shoe. I'd only heard about it in stories: this was what it was like to watch a man die.

"Minister."

When I heard my name, I was jolted back to myself, and everything rushed through me—the revival, the seat on the train, all that I had left behind and hadn't. I lowered the gun and there was a release, a collapse. The entire room jumped as the man's body fell, head crashing against the floor next to Carvall's fingertips. Then there was a long scream, and beneath it I heard Carvall whisper my name again.

I honestly thought there would be more blood. Some ran down the dead man's sleeves, forming a jagged line over the back of his hand into the webbing between his fingers, where it dripped through the slats in the floorboards. Still, it seemed like so little. Maybe that's why humanity is so fragile. Biologically, we should have more blood inside in order to endure.

I took a step backwards as the dark cherry pool crept closer to my shoes. One step turned into another, then another. It was as if I were trying to keep my balance, step after step to keep from falling backwards. The crowd parted behind me; no one wanted to touch me; everyone stayed away. I couldn't breathe. I turned towards the door and burst through it. As hard as I tried, or wanted, to let it go, the gun wouldn't fall from my hand; I can't remember when it finally did—whether it landed on wood or earth—or even what it felt like to have it burning in my hand one minute, then slipping away. I've never touched another gun since.

There wasn't enough air outside, either, so I started walking. I had to get back to Lanah and the Dawn Lightning. I had to. It was all I was. All I could think about. As I moved beyond the lights of the juke joint, a red glow caught my eye, flickering along both sides of the road that led out of the parking lot. The air thickened. Fires were burning in the dry grass. But I walked on alone, and soon the fields around me were engulfed in flames.

I didn't look behind me. I didn't look for Carvall or anyone. The smoke from the fires formed an acrid canopy over the road, the low sky a crematorium, ashes sticking on my suit jacket like snow, my body moving towards whatever peace and darkness was left in front of me. I wanted to run, but the weight of it all. Tatters of white cloth floated towards me, circled, then soared like apparitions. I tried not to look down as my shoes crunched the tiny stones, beetles, and centipedes in the road. Field mice by the thousands scurried from the ash and the flames, running across to find the same danger on the other side of the road, or heading for the darkness of the swamps ahead, like I was, or running towards me, past me, into the peeling heat.

Before she died, my grandmother told me that there were people made from fire. That's what dries them, but the rest of us—clay, still wet on the inside—take our time to truly harden.

The heat scorched my throat and lungs. I was parched, but I was convinced that every well near me was dry, filled with nothing but bones. On one side of the road a bare tree was filled with crows, but none of them flew away as I approached. The air shimmered. At first the smoke covered the stars like cataracts, but as I kept walking the acidity of the swamp air cleared it, and when I looked up at the sky again, the moon was renewed, laden, heavy, milky, slick, smooth. The soot and sweat dried on my skin. I wanted to close my eyes, but the cracks in the sclerae kept them open, and the last beautiful thing I saw was a grey-winged moth twisting in a breeze I couldn't feel.

I walked over cinder, brimstone, melting earth, and broken stones before the winds became even stronger, until I made my way to the station platform, now abandoned in the dead of night. No Divinion, Carvall, or other cousins followed. No one came looking for me. No one could help me. My skin was mist. I no longer had bones or water inside of me, only air. The Dawn Lightning, carrying everything that belonged to me which wasn't attached to my frame, was gone. Lanah was gone. My suitcase, with the rose petal inside, was gone. When I looked in either direction, it was too dark to see the tracks converging at the horizon. There was no more horizon, no sky, no future or past. I'd lost. I'd won. I waited for the moon to disappear, as it always eventually does, while every star in the pitch glared at me.

As I sat there on the platform, I thought about baptism by fire, then bodies floating out to sea—either on tall, beautiful ships in the middle of the ocean or from little sunken islands closer to shore. I thought of my daughter's body floating. I thought about other souls flying away. I tried to remember one of my daughter's songs—a chorus, a melody, one line of a verse, a single note—but nothing that came to my mind felt right. Around me the smell of smoke was still thick on the air. All the insects had stopped singing hymns. Still, no Carvall or Divinion. No soldiers. No brothers. No angels.

I started to laugh, hysterically, in the early morning, until the next train arrived. It was the last time in my entire life I've ever laughed that hard.

Eventually the carapace and chrysalis, ethereal and darkened, flaked off, and I couldn't remember a single drop of blood from the night earlier. I took a deep breath as a new train arrived, and I bought a new ticket and boarded as if I were a new person.

I took the first seat I could find. The unfamiliar air was cooling and scarring all at once. The new faces—whether ashen or glistening from sweat—appeared to be nothing more than clay masks drying in the emerging sunrise of the dirty windows. I spoke to no one. In the window across the aisle I thought I saw a comet, but it was only a streak of powder along the glass. I looked towards the burned and blackened fields in the distance, but they were too far away for me to see clearly. There were still some tall, white wisps of smoke, but I never learned what was burning to have caused them, and though I'm certain I smelled of smoke, and soot clung to my skin and clothes as the masks clung to their faces, no one asked my name or my situation. No one asked where I was headed. The train moved forward. The clouds were the color of dry teeth. In the field outside imagined I saw a chestnut horse, running beneath what was left of the moon.

I thought of an oil painting I once saw in a Saturday magazine. A deer, maybe the one I tried to kill in my youth, crossing a frozen lake. Back then I didn't know how heavy snow could be, or how it stung, and that picture made me envision its softness, its weightlessness until it touched the ground. I imagined my uncle in the picture, on the far side of the lake, the flame of my grandfather's red hot blood in his glowing eyes as the deer approached—the mist, carbon, and smoke from my uncle and the deer breathing, ice cracking into shards like knives under noctilucent clouds, wolves somewhere in the distance.

My father told me that once he and my uncle approached the South Carolina shore, the sea foam thickened, then turned to salt: so much salt that the boat they were in stopped, so much that they could scoop up the crystals in their hands. So much salt that they walked across it to get to the beach. All the salt from our ancestors who didn't make it across the seas. It was blinding. It made the distance so much farther than it originally seemed, their feet sinking deeper and deeper into it, every footfall only increasing their efforts, until eventually they reached the sands. Once there, they lay on their backs and looked up at the blue sky, then at the distance they'd traveled, and promised to never forget each other, and to endure.

✻ ⚹ ✻

So what if I told you that here—in those moments when the sky is the only wilderness left to our thoughts and dreams, when we've already made every other journey we were destined to make—is where God lives? What if that's my only story, the only secret I've ever had to tell? What if everything else is mere tautology? I'm much older now. Through it all, my memory has held fast to the one thing I have ever been sure of: that I survived. Like my grandmother, I tell stories to preserve the rest.

Eventually, one day, your anatomy starts to fail you. Your skin doesn't renew itself, your future becomes your epitaph, and you end up in a room that you'll never leave, where you spend time thinking about things and wondering why they're gone. My room has pipes and tubes and the best intentions connected to my body. My room has a doctor who visits once a day and a nurse who tells me, with a smile, that everything will be fine. A part of me is afraid that she is right. Everything is terribly comfortable and uncomfortable at the same time. For a few months I had a roommate who was a scientist, and who after retirement had worked as a locksmith at a kiosk in a supermarket parking lot because he liked the idea of having the keys to every mystery in his small booth. He died just recently, and the last thing he told me was how he'd never wanted his children to take care of him. Which made me realize that I've never taken care of anyone, or even really tried—or, if I did try, I didn't do a very good job.

For me now, the rectangle outside my window is the complete world. I'm comfortable with that, though I wonder how much of the rest is still burning. Through that window I watch the birth of clouds. Every evening, the world decays from blue to black to simply a reflection in the glass, and then bands of white light peel across the ceiling from the headlights of passing traffic. Then I close my eyes and sleep better than I ever have.

Sometimes, when I wake up, there will be a nurse or an orderly in my room. I'll say, "I want to tell you about my father." They'll smile politely and carefully ease away to other patients.

Other times they bring children to visit, who carry generic gifts made with their small hands and who've volunteered to sit with us for a few minutes. I try to entertain them with stories of my father and the sea monsters he encountered on the journey from his home island to the Carolina coast. Ferocious stingrays as long as buses, angry whales as wide as city blocks, sharks with enormous mouths and nineteen rows of razor teeth, mermaids, mile-long serpents, jellyfish the size of hot air balloons, sunken ships filled with treasure and the bodies of slaves. Some of the children believe me; others don't.

One even asked, "So, what happened to your uncle?"

I wanted to claim he'd wandered long patches of frozen, barren fields, never reaching the great western ocean. But in spite of all of the possibilities I'd envisioned, and in spite of all I've learned about ending a story with a distinct emotion, I simply answered, "I don't know."

As I sit here, staring at the trees I'll never touch, I often think of snow, and how much, over years of being here up North, I've learned to appreciate it. And the limbs of the trees that, in spite of the long winter months spent bowed under all that weight, still rise, bloom, continue. Beyond the trees blink the lights on the construction cranes reminding helicopters and low-flying airplanes that there is a future that is unavoidable.

I don't think much about the rest of my life after that train ride up the Eastern Seaboard, but I would like to consider my days happy ones—year after year, decade after decade of the planet and everything on it heating, cooling, freezing, then thawing through season upon season. In that time I bought a nice watch and kept it for years. I read book after book, with each one longing for the light from my father's old reading lamp to ease me through the pages. Once, a cat followed me home, and I took care of him for two decades until he died. In that time, he was the closest thing I had to a friend. I didn't make others. I told people that my "cousins" were coming to visit soon, so they stayed away; no one ever asked when. I never had another argument: that night in the juke joint was my last act of passion, the last bit of violence I've ever been involved in apart from a few brutal New York Januaries. After too many evenings of bread soup and cold sardines I went back into teaching. I taught algebra to the children of men who built skyscrapers in the early morning, who swept the empty streets at night, who carried the steel used to form the city's core, who dug holes for lampposts and telephone poles so we could all connect to each other a little better, who cleaned the gutters with dark fingers and held tiny hands in those same fingers before bedtimes.

So I'd like to think that I've influenced the world somehow, if only from afar; none of us expected the roads up north to bubble with sugar and gold, but what we had seemed better than what was even possible before. Some of my students became successful enough to never have to come home. Some became surgeons, astronomers, and scientists, so you'd think that by mere association I'd have a better understanding of how to cut away the parts of myself that I don't need any longer. To remove the parts that continue to spread infection and hurl them towards the evening skies to dissolve among the stars. One became a linguist and taught me about the concept of *sankofa*; another became a geologist and taught me about *sastrugi*. The physicists taught me about time and eternity; the cardiologists taught me about the human heart. On my own I learned some astrology and phrenology, but I don't believe the stars have any secrets left, and in the end bumps on the head are just damage.

I never remarried or fell in love again. But I've watched the sun drop below the tops of buildings, below a hovering kestrel or the flights of sparrows, as the sky slowly darkens. That's romance. I've seen elephants, majestic, in cages, with the saddest eyes I've ever witnessed on any being. I've watched children count fallen leaves. I've seen women wearing pearls and diamonds as protection. I've heard eruptions of laughter so boisterous and true that it shook windows, street lamps, and hearts; I, myself, have even laughed so fully at times that it didn't sound like my own voice. Nothing like my laughter on the train platform that night, but much more enjoyable. I've seen two people fall in love and not even know it. I've looked for Lanah on the silver screen. I've sat in movie theaters where lovers clutch each other tightly, each afraid that the other might float away, while on the screen we watch the imaginations of people we'll never meet coalesce with our own. The greatest of human gifts is the ability to project a self-image larger than ourselves across a desert, an ocean, or a canvas. All of these things, and more, I wanted for my daughter.

Since that night, ages ago in the juke joint, I've never raised my voice. And to this day, I've never screamed. Or cried.

I just lived, then fell into a quiet that I never emerged from. I've decayed nicely, and my apparitions and I have come to an understanding. No regrets. With time you learn to make peace with everything rotting inside you. When you've reached my age, you've already become all that you're going to be. Whenever any pain does rise it always lingers longer than I expect it to, like it wants to remind me of something I already understand, but I breathe through it, and eventually it fades like everything else.

I've learned that my father was right; our planet is sinking. Orbits and rotations degrade, yet it's still a little over three thousand six hundred miles from New York to Paris. I wonder, if Lanah ever made it there, how she's spent the years. Some quiet days I would look up Parisian newspapers at the library just to see if there was a picture of her. I never found one, and I never went searching for her myself. Like-wise, she never came searching for me—or if she did, she probably stopped trying well before I did. The earth is long.

Vision degrades, but I can still see her face. I think of her every day, even though, try as I might, I can't envision what life we might have had together. Instead, I think of her smile, her hair, and how much she illuminated every-thing around her. I've never looked at anyone since the way I looked at her. I think of Ronalda Lawson, too, though not quite as often. They were both beautiful in their own way. I wouldn't say, though, that I loved either of them; you can't fall in love with anything that's so distant, and always has been.

By now, all of the stars in the sky have settled into their dance, memorized its steps and followed them; by now, both women are so far away that they are little more than fragments of a remembered image.

Someone once told me that the greatest gift one person can give another is a kiss. I gave kisses to my wife, and my daughter, but those were the last, besides in dreams, that I have ever felt.

After telling that story of my grandfather, my grand-mother would remind me that whatever we love, we bury, partially or whole, hoping to be able to dig it up and love it again someday.

But—like Lanah, unlike Lot's wife—I'm wise enough to not turn back for what I've left. To me, Carvall and Divin-ion never left that bar that night, so their future is rarely in my thoughts. They are frozen, yet will dissolve. They will vanish. The rest is just scripture.

❋ ⚓ ❋

No part of me has ever regretted leaving the South, and I've never tried to reshape it in my mind and make it a place better or worse than it was. In the hard northern winters I sometimes miss my grandmother's quilt, but I've convinced myself that's simply a desire for familiar warmth over an easy department store purchase. I do miss bottle trees. Sometimes, in summer, I miss how the grasses there would whisper the names of those I'd lost, but those voices were never anything more than my imagination. As much as even I wanted to stay with Divinion's family, I, like my father, left them all to drown. I left everyone down there to drown, and I'm sure that, had I stayed, I would be dead already—devoured by the sea or rotting on the surface of the earth. I'm not brave. Up here, in this city with more steel and stone than I could have imagined, things are more comfortable.

When you get to the end of the tracks, they no longer converge on a single sharp point. Instead the lines open up and widen the closer you get to stopping. I've aged. No, I've gotten old. And here I am going blind, with the diabetes surging through my blood destined to take the rest of me away.

My students who became optometrists claim that eyesight blurring and fading over time is the reason one sees ghosts when older, optic nerves tricking the mind with images that aren't there, but I believe it's simply the spirits catching up to us. It's with my mind's eye, in that little twinkle right beyond the periphery, that I see the clearest now. Some days I sit in my armchair, with the door to my small room open, and wait for Carvall to walk in: big grin stretching from cheekbone to cheekbone, handing me one of his letters as if, all along, he was writing it for me. But he has yet to haunt that doorway.

I'll wait. I'll dream. I have enough time now to explain to him that maybe those Black soldiers left him on that European field as a kindness, an act of mercy, to save him from the horror of still being less than once he returned home, in spite of his uniform. Maybe they hoped that, if he lived, he would be treated beautifully somewhere else, and if he died, after all of the sorrow, he would be honored as a hero, as he deserved, even if it were by those on a distant shore.

Standing on the proper coast, you can see the sunrise, but often that daybreak only reminds you of where you aren't. I never learned how to swim, and I've never been on a boat, but I could have walked to France had I truly wanted. There's always frozen salt water capping the tips of the planet, and nowadays there is certainly enough blood and salt in the oceans everywhere to support my weight. No one I care about, or am interested in, can ever be more than twenty-five thousand miles away—eight thousand, if I were to travel through the new, wet, still-beating center of the earth. I should have kept my father's almanac just in case.

Once up north, I stopped going to church, but some Sundays I would walk past the storefront services to the beaches, where I faced down the winds and blowing silica grains to gaze over the sleepless Atlantic and the continents beyond. I collected beach glass worn smooth by ancient sands; I imagined slave bodies washed onto beaches this far north. I wanted to melt into some encroaching spirit of salt, but as the waves licked my shoes I would step back more and more—I'd gone as far as my wanderlust would carry me, it seems—until I was in my apartment again, dreaming, pressing my daughter's picture to my heart, listening to distant rhythms through a small transistor radio. Afterwards I would talk to my wife, tell her about my day, and we would dance until the city lights died for the approaching morning. If I closed my eyes I could feel the water rise against my bare feet and then ebb away like the years, never returning. Sometimes, toward morning, our daughter would join us, her feet on top of mine as we spun until the music drifted into static and I drifted into arid silence, into bed, then to sleep. It would have been nice to have either of them to watch the burial of the stars with.

At times I remember so little of my journey; other times I remember it all. Here's what I can't forget. That wounded night alone on the train platform, with no clouds to block the theater of constellations, the moon sitting in judgement, ringed by her court of sharp stars. Everything, my entire life beforehand and all I'd known in it, was comprised of some degree of heat; even after a long South Carolina rain I would dry so quickly that I barely shivered. But the cold from the train station that late night has stayed with me more than any northern winter, like some part of me is now frozen, crystalline, petrified.

I haven't felt warmth since that night.

Me, at the edges of things. I thought I liked that about my life, how seeing all of the blades kept me from being sliced in two.

But here's what I ask myself: Am I any different now than I would have been had I not pulled that trigger?

No matter. The world, I know now, is designed to survive you. I figure I spent too much time running away from things I should have been running towards, but maybe running, creating that distance, is what life is all about.

Yesterday I taught someone how to walk again. We were in the rehabilitation area and I was watching him, a man about ten years my senior, shuffling his feet, leaning forward but not truly progressing.

"It's simple," I reminded him. "You lift one foot, put it in front of the other, and then repeat until you're someplace else. Someplace you'd rather be. It's about renewal."

You move forward. Each footfall presses the ground, dust you can't see scatters, and the earth pushes against you until you move ahead.

I used to believe that travel was a form of destruction, and that it was much easier to destroy than to create, but here's what you never tell yourself enough: destruction is a myth, because things never truly end. Particles rearrange and vibrate and dance elsewhere, as we settle into dust, salt, *toujours*, *kal*, next.

About the Author

ORIGINALLY FROM BUFFALO, and currently living in Seattle, Stacy D. Flood has had work published and performed nationally as well as in the Puget Sound area. He received his MFA in Creative Writing from San Francisco State University and has been an artist-in-residence at DISQUIET in Lisbon, as well as The Millay Colony of the Arts. In addition, he is the recipient of the Gregory Capasso Award in Fiction from the University at Buffalo, along with a Getty Fellowship to the Squaw Valley Community of Writers.